I0726384

His Majesty's Hounds– Book 1

Sweet and Clean Regency Romance

Claiming the Heart of a Duke

Arietta Richmond

Dreamstone Publishing © 2016

www.dreamstonepublishing.com

ISBN: 1925499154

ISBN-13: 978-1-925499-15-5

Books by Arietta Richmond

His Majesty's Hounds

Claiming the Heart of a Duke

Intriguing the Viscount

Giving a Heart of Lace (a prequel to Winning the Merchant Earl)

Being Lady Harriet's Hero

Enchanting the Duke (coming soon)

Redeeming the Marquess (coming soon)

Healing Lord Barton (coming soon)

Winning the Merchant Earl (coming soon)

Loving the Bitter Baron (coming soon)

Rescuing the Countess (coming soon)

Attracting the Spymaster (coming soon)

The Derbyshire Set

A Gift of Love (Prequel short story)

A Devil's Bargain (Prequel short story - coming soon)

The Earl's Unexpected Bride

The Captain's Compromised Heiress

The Viscount's Unsuitable Affair

The Count's Impetuous Seduction

The Rake's Unlikely Redemption

The Marquess' Scandalous Mistress

A Remembered Face (Bonus short story – coming soon)

The Marchioness' Second Chance (coming soon)

A Viscount's Reluctant Passion (coming soon)

Lady Theodora's Christmas Wish

The Duke's Improper Love (coming soon)

Other Books

The Scottish Governess (coming soon)

The Earl's Reluctant Fiancée (coming soon)

The Crew of the Seadragon's Soul Series, (coming soon - a set of 10 linked novels)

Dedication

For everyone who had the grace to be patient while this book, and every other book that I have written, were coming into existence, who provided cups of tea, and food, when the writing would not let me go, and endured countless times being asked for opinions.

For the readers who will come to know these characters, in this new series, well, as they have come to know the characters in my other series well, and who inspire me to continue, by buying my books!

For my growing team of beta readers and advance reviewers – it's thanks to you that others can enjoy these books in the best presentation possible!

And for all the writers of Regency Historical Romance, whose books I read, who inspired me to write in this fascinating period.

ARIETTA RICHMOND

Chapter One

Having broken his fast at the inn that morning, Hunter Barrington, tenth Duke of Melton, had decided that he would ride for the last leg of his journey, because he was heartily sick of the stuffy carriage and of his valet's mournful mien.

This worthy, whom he had hired following his friend Raphael's advice (for it seemed that his business was a source of excellent information, not just imported goods), had vainly tried to turn him into a dandy during their short stay in London. Hunter smiled thinking of Bulwick's dismay when he had flatly refused to use the cane that Bulwick had tried to foist upon him, or to buy the inordinate number of fobs, which it was fashionable to attach to one's watch chain. After years in the field, his taste in dress was so simple that it could be called austere. Not so long ago, a day with clean clothes had been worth savouring, so all of this fuss seemed rather ridiculous to him.

Poor Bulwick had been horrified when he had declared his intention to ride.

"You can't possibly do that, my Lord," he had whispered.

"You will reach Meltonbrook Chase in a dishevelled and mussed condition. You will get a head cold, of a certainty. And, my Lord, if I may presume to comment further, the road is in very bad condition and frozen all over."

"Fustian!"

Hunter had exclaimed, shrugging away his valet's concern.

"It will do me good. Look after my luggage, Felton. I'm off."

The road, in his opinion, was quite good – certainly a vast improvement on trampled battlefields and roads in a war zone!

So, without further ado, he had swung onto his horse, leaving the bewildered valet with his mouth still open in protest.

For the first few miles, the ride had been exhilarating. Warmly clad in his greatcoat, beaver hat and fur lined gloves, astride his dapple grey stallion, he had delighted in the cold wind and in the speed-blurred landscape, as he let the stallion run off his energy.

The feeling of freedom, however, did not last long and had already vanished when Meltonbrook Chase appeared in the distance.

It was the first time he had seen his family estate since his father, the late Duke, had purchased a commission for him, as was traditional for a second son.

Hunter could remember, perfectly well, his father's stern admonitions, imparted before sending him on his way to London, and hence to the Peninsular and war.

"Honour first of all, my son. Honour means more than life to our family. Never tarnish it, never demean yourself, never show a streak of the yellow. Remember, an officer and a nobleman must be an example for his men. England must stand against the French tyrant. Your commitment must be wholehearted. Your days as a dissipated and wild young buck have ended. Do you understand?"

'I thought I understood, Father, but I didn't. Only later, I did. Oh, yes, later I understood, all too well, what you meant.' Hunter's thought was wry, and a little sad.

He was so absorbed in his musings that he was barely registering the landscape. It took some time for him to realise that he was inside Meltonbrook Chase's expansive park. He reined in his horse, and stopped to look at the wintry landscape around him.

The silence was profound, broken only by the cawing of a crow, somewhere in the woods, and by the soft murmuring of the nearby brook.

The grounds were immaculate under the heavy pall of snow, the ice-traced tall poplars, which surrounded the lake, shining like silver filigree under the setting sun's slanting rays.

"I'm home." he thought, steeling himself for his first meeting with his family, after so many years.

Riding into the deserted stable yard, it seemed surreal that he was actually here – and even more surreal that his father and brother were gone, that all of this was his now.

He dismounted, the icy gravel crunching under his feet, as a brawny groom, in a leather coat, came running toward him.

"Master Hunter! Master Hunter! Is it you? Is it really you? At long last you're home again!" The man suddenly checked and lowered his head.

"Begging your pardon, Your Grace. I've been overfamiliar, but me happiness made me tongue run away with me, it did, old fool that I am."

"Never you mind, Nick. Master Hunter it is, if you wish it, as long as you keep it just between us. You know how stuffy my mother can be… Now, this is Nuage…." he gestured to the horse, which snuffled curiously at the old groom. "I bought him in France, and a valiant fellow he is. Take good care of him, will you? Go with Nick, my boy, he's a good one."

Nick stroked the horse's silky coat and took the reins.

"Always been a good judge of horseflesh, Master Hunter. Since you was a stripling, you was. Come along Nuage, a good rubdown is what you need right now. And what about some clean straw to lie on and some oats to chew?" Talking to the horse, the head groom disappeared around the corner toward the stable, as the carriage, bearing his valet, and his meagre luggage, drew up before the house.

Nerissa looked at her reflection in the tall mirror and sighed.

She would never be an Incomparable, and that was that. Her colouring was all wrong, she was too tall and her face was too angular.

In the pale pastel colours that were deemed fashionable for young ladies, she faded into insignificance.

She sighed again, thinking of her sister Maria, an acknowledged Beauty, who had cut a triumphant swathe through the *ton* during the previous Season. It had been fashionable to be in love with Maria, with her flashing amber eyes, rich auburn hair and flawless creamy complexion.

Thus, Maria had had the opportunity of choosing from amongst a veritable army of suitors and was now betrothed - very advantageously betrothed, to be sure, to a wealthy Earl, to their parents' delight.

Donning her fur lined pelisse and her velvet bonnet, Nerissa crossed the hall and stepped into the carriage with her maid, bound to Meltonbrook Chase, where she was to have tea with her bosom bow Alyse, the Duke of Melton's daughter.

No, not daughter, sister, she amended her thought. Hunter was Duke, now, after the untimely demise of his father and his elder brother.

She blushed. They hoped that Hunter would be home soon, for he had sent his family a message from London, but with the deep snow on the roads, he was likely delayed.

Would he recognise her? She did not think so. He had had scant interest to spare for her, to begin with, when he was a young man just back from his term in Oxford, and she was just a shy ten year old, all angles and elbows and not even a promise of feminine allure.

Nerissa leaned back on the carriage seat, closing her eyes. *'Much good it does me to wool-gather like that'*, she chided herself. *'I'll be lucky if I don't find myself married to some gouty old man before the Season is over.'*

She shivered, and not because of the sharp wind blowing and howling through the naked trees.

~~~~~~~~~

As Hunter approached the door, the butler, a delighted expression lighting his usually impassive features, opened it. Immediately regaining his formal demeanour, Jermyn schooled his expression to a more serious face, better suited to the Butler of a great house.

"Welcome home, my lord. The ladies are in the drawing room. Follow me, please."

"No need, Jermyn, I know the way", answered Hunter, secretly amused by the butler's display of self-restraint, and almost ran to the drawing room doors, suddenly unable to wait any longer to see his family.

He opened the doors, and an instant of shocked silence followed his entrance.

Hunter scanned the tableau – a morning visit frozen before him. All of his family were there (although part of his mind still expected to see his father and Richard as well), and there was someone else.

A woman he did not know, a woman who was more beautiful than any he had seen.

She had burnished golden hair, surrounding her face with a profusion of waves and ringlets, a honey and gold complexion; long, almond shaped green gold eyes, fringed by thick burnished golden eyelashes and emphasized by high cheekbones, and a tall, shapely body.
~~~~~~~~~

The only feature detracting from perfection, but greatly adding to character, was a rather large, mobile mouth, much more capable of expressing feelings (and temper, he suspected!) than a proper prim little rosebud. He was captivated. Her eyes met his across the room, and for a moment, everything else faded away.

He was brought back to the moment when the silence was broken by his sister Alyse, who cried out: "Hunter! Hunter, you are back! Is it really you, Hunter?" and, without any further ado, threw herself at him. His eye contact with the woman was broken, and he forgot her in the chaos that followed.

Hunter's mother, the Duchess Louisa, half-fainting, reclined on the sofa, fanning herself and calling for her vinaigrette. His sister Sybilla, almost jigged around the table, before forcing herself to behave with greater propriety. His brother, Charles, obviously tried to be the cool gentleman, but could not help but step forward and embrace Hunter, his eyes shining with held back tears.

"At long last, my son," sobbed his mother.

"Come here, and let me look at you. Last time I saw you, you were a boy. Now you are a man. And what a man! Your father, God rest his soul, would be so proud of you..."

Moved despite himself, Hunter gathered his weeping mother into his arms.

"Shush, Mother, I'm here to stay. I'm so sorry I was not here when it would have really mattered. I feel that I have failed you all, yet it was at the time of Waterloo, and I did not even hear the news for months! I'm so sorry..."

The Duchess brushed her tears impatiently aside.

"I'm a foolish old woman, my son. This is not a time for weeping, but a time for rejoicing. God knows, we have been mourning long enough. And look who is here, Hunter. Do you remember Lady Nerissa Loughbridge, Lord Chester's youngest daughter?"

A faint recollection of a meddlesome brat, always trying to follow him around, vaguely stirred in Hunter's memory.

He turned his head and froze again, caught by her appearance.

Brat? She was not a brat anymore, she was a woman, and a very beautiful woman at that, more so because of her unusual colouring.

It was all he could do not to stare at her with his mouth agape. He tried to react in some polite way, and smiled, suddenly recalling one of Nerissa's youthful misdeeds.

"Nerissa? Was it you who hid inside your brother Kevin's portmanteau, because you wanted to come with us when we went to our hunting lodge near Cottesmore? And did we not discover you because you sneezed? Do you remember, Charles?"

Nerissa had not heard a single word.

Hunter's sudden appearance had completely stunned her.

All her childhood emotions flooded back, crowding her mind, amplified with new meaning and significance. A rosy blush washed upon her face as she dared to smile back.

"She's not a child anymore, Hunter," broke in Alyse.

"She is a dear friend to us all, and I really don't know how we would have managed without her. She is a sensible young woman, with a good head on her shoulders, and she gave us invaluable help when Mother was so ill after…" Alyse's voice faltered "…after the accident…"

Hunter looked at his family: his sisters, pretty, vivacious, eager to try out their wings during the London Season, his mother, with her gentle face marked by loss and sorrow, his brother, suddenly scowling and dark browed, and the enchanting stranger in their midst. He felt rather like he had stepped into the centre of a whirlwind.

Suddenly he felt mortally tired, in dire need of rest and solitude.

He went to his mother and kissed her gently on her cheek.

"Will you please excuse me, Mother? I have had a long and tiring journey and I'm much fatigued. I believe that, if you will forgive me, I will have a bath drawn and a tray sent to my room. I am not really up to a formal supper. Tomorrow, we can all begin to catch up."

"But of course, my dear. How thoughtless of me not having foreseen your needs… my happiness at seeing you again quite overwhelmed me. I have not all my wits about me, I'm sure… Jermyn, please, see His Grace to his apartments and make sure that his valet attends him."

"Yes, my lady. Please follow me, Your Grace."

To his chagrin, Jermyn did not lead Hunter to his bachelor's quarters as he had unthinkingly expected, but to his father's apartments.

That was the precise moment at which the full import of his new condition crashed in upon him like a dark and overwhelming wave.

He was the Duke of Melton.

Not his father, nor his elder brother, both now dead after a freak carriage accident. Himself.

He had not wanted it, he had not coveted it, truth to tell, he had no idea how to go about being a Duke, but there it was, with all its implications and obligations, including the need to marry, and to sire heirs to the title.

It was like a bad dream, but it was not going to disappear at dawn.

Chapter Two

Hunter rode along a rutted track, across a barren and ravaged landscape, under a dark and menacing sky. The stench of burned and rotting flesh, of death and decay was all pervading, a leaden overcoat on his shoulders. Far away, one could hear the great, long-distance artillery guns roaring, more like a muted vibration than a real noise.

Around him, there was nothing but destruction - bloated carcasses, untended fields, ruined buildings and skeletal trees - where once cattle had grazed, wheat had ripened and orchards had blossomed. Suddenly something, a white rag fluttering in the rank wind, half-hidden by the ditch, attracted his attention. He was drawn toward it, almost without volition, but stopped dead in horror when he was near enough to see.

Beatriz lay lifeless, among rubble and sundry discarded items, her skin beaten and bruised with the imprint of vicious hands, her body broken and bloody, her mouth still half open in a hopeless scream, her lovely dark eyes fixed, and staring in a desperate appeal into the eternity of death.

Beatriz. His love.

Beatriz, on whose grave he had cried until his throat was raw. Beatriz, whom war had wrenched from him and who had died alone, in shame and terror, ravished by French troops in rout after the battle of Vitoria.

Beatriz, one of the countless casualties of war.

Suddenly, something shifted, and a flickering image of another face, in a soft green and golden light, like a sunbeam on new leaves, flashed into his mind, and broke the grip of the dream.

Hunter woke, drenched in cold sweat, lurching to his feet, his heart beating wildly against his ribcage.

At first, he stood bewildered, unable to recognise his surroundings, still gripped by the horror of his recurring nightmare, then, gradually, he calmed down, his heartbeat steadied and his anguish receded.

It was not real. He had never seen Beatriz like that, he had only seen her grave, been told of her death. He did not know, could never know, how terrible that death had been – but his imagination was all too able to present him with the ghastly possibilities. As it did – almost every night.

Completely awake now, he drank deeply of the water, which Bulwick had thoughtfully provided, in a carafe on the side table. He went to the window, opened the heavy velvet drapes, and peered outside.

It was still dark, but a faint rosy shade began to colour the East. No question of going back to sleep, now. Hunter was sure that Nick was already up and going.

He would look for the old groom and wipe away the last of the nightmare, listening to Nick relating everything that had been going on here, during his long absence from home.

~~~~~~~~

Lady Louisa Barrington, Duchess of Melton, looked critically at her face in the mirror, while her young maid, Prudence, was arranging her hair under a flattering beribboned lace cap.

"You look yourself again, my lady, if I may say so. You have filled up a bit and your eyes… But now", she went on briskly "his Lordship is back home again and everything will be all right, will it not, my Lady?"

Lady Melton smiled. She had known Prudence since her birth, the daughter of a respectable but impoverished family, and was used to her artless demeanour. And the girl was right. For the first time since the accident, she could look at herself with some satisfaction, and at the future with some hope.

She closed her eyes, remembering the mindless terror that had gripped her when the careening coach, driven by some drunken lout, had suddenly appeared around the bend. The horses had reared, neighing, and the heavier vehicle had smashed full into their light travelling carriage, with a sickening noise of crushed wood. That sound was the last thing she could recall before oblivion had claimed her.

Louisa shook herself out of her brooding. Time to start the new day and to get to know, again, her own son – so much time had passed - she wondered what sort of man he had become.

There was so much to be said and done.
~~~~~~~~

She sighed. Some of what had to be said would not be pleasant. Her late elder son, Richard, heir presumptive to the title, had not been wise. Handsome and debonair, always exuding charm, a redoubtable Corinthian, able to spar with Gentleman Jackson himself, and to feather angles with his curricle, he had also been a reckless gambler and had entertained questionable relationships with ladies of dubious virtue. His father, the late Duke, had been so inordinately proud of his heir, that he had never checked or restrained him.

"Don't you fret, my boy" he had indulgently told Charles, his hard working, serious third born, when he had shown his father the heavy dent that Richard's expenses were making in the estate's revenues.

"Let him be, he will calm down in time and, anyway, we can afford it, can't we?"

'Well, we are not destitute,' she thought, *'and the estate is vastly profitable, thanks to Charles' thrifty management, but, with two dowries to provide for, a mansion in London to keep up, and a living to arrange for Charles, if he decides to enter the Church (although that seems rather less likely now)… things need to change. It is, truly, not seemly for Charles to act as his brother's steward – regardless of the cost, an estate manager must be employed. And, as Hunter really must marry, and get himself an heir, a good dowry would not come amiss, now, would it?'*

~~~~~~~~~

In a few days, a routine, of a sort, had been established.
~~~~~~~~~

Hunter would wake at dawn, after a restless night plagued by nightmares, go down to the stables and have a chat with Nick, take a brisk walk in the park and then break his fast, with his family, in the small dining room.

It was a cosy and intimate room which he liked infinitely better than the formal dining room, with its long table, musty hangings and depressing centrepieces.

His mother would tell him about his neighbours, and expound on her plans for the coming Season; his sisters would laugh and chatter and talk of French couturierès, balls and routs; his brother would prose on about the estate, the tenants and the improvements he had thought of. Hunter would listen to everybody, nod genially, let the flow of conversation dance around him, and reprove himself for his lack of interest.

After having dealt with decisions which entailed life or death, for much of his adult life, he could not help but feel that there was a slight lack of import, or even sense, in the topics in which his family – as dear as everyone was to him – seemed so absorbed.

Life as Colonel Lord Barrington had been much harsher, but much simpler, than life as His Grace the Duke of Melton.

Hunter soon realised that his mother wanted him married tout de suite, possibly before the Season ended, and preferably to a young lady with a fat dowry.

He found this an appalling prospect, because, even if not averse to marriage in principle, he did not want to be rushed, neither did he want somebody else to choose for him.

His mind felt scarred, still torn by everything that he had seen and done – and he was not about to explain anything of that, to anyone. It was still too sensitive a topic, and his nightmares unsettled him more than he cared to admit.

Perusing his library, he had found a book of Ancient Greek poetry, and read a fragment by Sappho, with which he felt a total affinity:

"Like wild gales, sweeping desolate mountains

uprooting oaks

Eros harrows my heart

sweet, bitter, indomitable wild beast…"

Beatriz was still an indelible, aching wound. He did not want to suffer again. He did not want to lose his heart to somebody who could tear it asunder.

He wanted an affectionate, companionable marriage. He wanted to be friends with his wife. He wanted a sensible, cool-headed young woman, not some vapid, giggling miss or some haughty high-flier.

One afternoon, while he was walking, brooding and trying to sort out his feelings, full of a sense of guilt, that he, as the Duke, could not bring himself to care, more, for the management of his estates, he wandered away from his usual path and found himself deep inside his neighbour's park.

Looking around, at first he did not understand where he was: the natural woods of the park had progressively given way to a more structured growth.

The park seemed larger than he remembered, with cunningly planted thickets, graceful avenues flanked by stately trees, cosy nooks, elegant fountains, well designed flowerbeds and herbaceous borders. Even now, in the depths of the winter, it was not difficult to imagine a profusion of bright colours vying with each other to the beholder's delight.

He remembered the park as he had known it during his childhood: a fascinating tangle of trees, creepers and weeds, which could well become a mysterious jungle, where his friend Kevin, Lord Chester's son, his brothers and himself, would hunt for wild beasts, find hidden treasures and fight warlike natives.

Lord Chester must have hired a new head gardener, Hunter mused. The place had improved beyond recognition.

His senses, honed by times when the ability to hear insignificant noises could make the difference between life and death, perceived a slight rustle, as if something were moving between the winter bare bushes, and he stepped abruptly past the branches.

To his chagrin, he found himself at less than a foot's distance from Lady Nerissa, who could not hold back a soft whimper of startlement at his sudden appearance.

"I am sorry, Lady Nerissa", he spoke softly, almost as startled as she appeared to be. "Did I scare you?"

She smiled, lowering her eyes. He found himself disappointed that she had veiled their green-gold depths from his sight.

"Not at all, my Lord. However, I should not be here on my own, without a chaperone. Please excuse me, I must go back at once."

Her beauty seemed to burn like a flame against the frozen background, composing a jewelled symphony of brilliant shades: gold, silver, coral, aquamarine, mother of pearl, as the cool winter light reflected from the warmth of her skin.

"Nerissa!" Hunter exclaimed, loath to let her go. "Lady Nerissa, we are old friends and neighbours, are we not? Surely nobody could object to our exchanging a few words in an open place, during a casual meeting. I am the meekest and most inoffensive of gentlemen, I do assure you!"

Nerissa looked at Hunter under her lowered lashes. He gave an impression of energy and passion kept on a tight leash, like a wild horse straining at restraints. His deep sapphire eyes flashed in a countenance darkened by many seasons spent in warmer climates, his firm mouth and strong chin bespoke character and courage, his lean, hard body and his long, sensitive fingers, made her feel... she could not even name those feelings.

No, he was not inoffensive, he was very dangerous, much too dangerous for her own peace of mind, for she had discovered, to her chagrin, that she found him just as attractive now, as she had as an infatuated ten year old.

She should go away, but she could not. Mesmerised by his smile, she smiled in return.

"Just a few minutes, then. Let's walk, it is too cold, and the ground too damp, to sit anyway..."

They walked for a while, making small talk, stealing surreptitious glances at each other, laughing without a real reason, somehow prisoners of the strange enchantment of their unexpected meeting.

Nerissa felt as if they were inside a fragile, iridescent bubble and, at the same time, she clearly perceived the terrible impropriety of their situation. Even so, the rebellious mood which had made her fly from home and seek the haven of her beloved park persisted, and made her feel stubborn and daring, enjoying Hunter's company with a carefree elation.

But, while she was tucking a stray, wind-tossed tress under her bonnet, the portfolio she was carrying opened and the sheets inside fluttered and fell to the ground.

Hunter was quick to stoop and help her to collect them, but was very surprised when he discovered that they were not the kind of artwork that one was used to expect from a young lady - pastels, gouaches, flowers and landscapes, painstakingly rendered, dull and respectable - but something completely different, something resembling, strangely enough, the neat battle plans he had so often pored over during his soldiering days.

Nerissa blushed a deep crimson, and almost wrenched the sheets from his hand. The laughing, relaxed mood of the last hour disappeared in a moment, and she was suddenly tense and distant.

"Thank you, Lord Melton," Nerissa whispered.

"I must go now. Goodbye..." and turning quickly, she almost ran away, leaving Hunter bewildered and wondering what all that had been about.

Chapter Three

Nerissa arrived home flushed and breathless, her hair dishevelled, her bonnet askew. The footman, opening the door, told her the family was in the morning room, waiting for afternoon tea to be served, and Nerissa nodded and ran lightly upstairs to restore her appearance lest she incur in her mother's displeasure - a frequent enough occurrence, she conceded with a wry smile.

It seemed to Nerissa she was hearing her mother's high pitched voice: *"You look like a vulgar hoyden, my daughter. It is highly unseemly for a well-bred young lady to go gallivanting around without an escort, even in one's own parkland. One never knows whom or what one could meet. A lady's reputation is as beautiful and as fragile as a crystal bauble: once besmirched, it is impossible to restore. I will not have a soiled dove for a daughter - have I made myself clear, Nerissa?"*

Nerissa sighed. Of course Maria, the perfect Maria, would never have behaved in such a reprehensible fashion…

Nerissa took particular care to remove every sign of her escapade. She changed her slightly muddy boots for a pair of simple black slippers, she carefully coiled her hair, she smoothed her pale blue gown and righted the simple golden chain around her neck. A quick look in the mirror told her that she was as properly turned out as she could possibly be, and she headed to the morning room, where her family was waiting. Her mother looked her over from head to toe, as if trying – Nerissa thought - to find fault with her.

"You are late, as usual." Lady Chester said, in a languid resigned tone. "Am I allowed to enquire as to what kept you from joining us earlier?"

"I was reading, Mother", Nerissa answered quietly.

"You'll do better to try to improve your accomplishments, Nerissa. Gentlemen ridicule bluestockings, but admire ladies who can play pleasantly, sing sweetly, and dance with elegance and restraint. Young ladies should be pliant yet virtuous, gay yet innocent. I've told you so, many times, but you do not seem to take my kindly lectures to heart... You will not – alas - be noticed for your beauty, my daughter - you must be noticed for your sweet temper and pleasant disposition."

Nerissa suppressed, with a shudder, the highly improper thought crossing her mind - had she been a gentleman, far from being charmed, she would have been bored stiff by such a milksop. Maria, who was embroidering a linen cloth, a long strand of rainbow hued silk streaming from her deft fingers, looked up from the frame and smiled slightly.

"I feel, Mama, that embroidery is the most feminine of arts, do you not think so?"

Lady Chester beamed at her elder daughter.

"Now, this is exactly the kind of charming remark suitable for a young lady. No wonder you did so well, Maria. If only your sister would heed me…"

The Honourable Kevin Loughbridge, Lord Chester's only son and heir, who was perusing The Sporting Magazine's latest issue, rolled his eyes and winked at Nerissa. Their age and gender notwithstanding, they had always been close allies and accomplices, each one aiding and abetting the other's mischief.

Nerissa repressed a very unfeminine spurt of laughter and concentrated on sipping her tea in the most genteel fashion.

Lord Chester looked at her with a fierce scowl – it was an expression which her father had perfected.

"Now that the Duke is back home, you stay away from Meltonbrook Chase, my girl, do you hear me? I do not want you to consort with him, or to be seen with him, even with his mother and sisters in attendance. I don't want to hear your name associated with his in any fashion. Always been wild to a fault, that one, until my old friend Raymond – God rest his soul! - packed him off to the Army. I don't think they succeeded in straightening him out, mind you. He probably spent his time abroad preening in his regimentals and making it up to strump… ahem… to loose women. Goes against my grain, to see his father's place so unworthily occupied. Now, Charles, Raymond's youngest boy, that's a fine steady young man. Too bad he is not the heir. Good head on his shoulders, good feel for the land."

Nerissa looked surreptitiously at her father, her rebellious thoughts saying things that she could not say aloud.

"What would you say, Sir, if you knew that I spent at least one whole, unchaperoned hour with that very same despicable character, the Duke of Melton? And what would my mother think if she knew about my dream of being a garden designer? Of planning and building beautifully landscaped parks, a pleasure for the senses, as well as for the mind? Or, worse, if she knew that I am actually the one who has planned our park? That the improvements she brags about to Lady Emerson, or to Mrs. Radclyffe, the Rector's wife, are not of the head gardener's, but of my own contriving?"

Nerissa sighed, simply nodded, and picked up, from the side table, the embroidery that she had been, for some weeks now, failing to do.

Her father barely noticed. After having thus vented his spleen, Lord Chester stood up and motioned Kevin to follow him.

"Let's have a look at that nag you bought, my son. They probably cheated you out of most of your money, don't you know? Let's leave this gaggle of females to their own devices..."

Three days had passed since his meeting with Nerissa and, even if Hunter had often strolled near the place where he had run into her, he had not seen more of the elusive and enchanting young lady.

The day before, he had gone with his mother, his brother and his sisters to pay his respects to Lord Chester and his family, but he could not help noticing the cold, formal demeanour of the Viscount and his lady wife. It was clear that the stiff-necked aristocrat had not forgiven him his youthful pranks and follies, which, Hunter had to admit, had often been outrageous enough. It seemed that Lord Chester could not conceive that six years at war might change a man.

Nerissa had not been there. She was, as Lady Chester had graciously deigned to explain, with a group of ladies, led by the Rector's wife, who had gone to bestow hand knitted scarves and socks upon the deserving poor down at the village.

"My Maria would have gone with them, tender hearted creature that she is, but I would not have it", she had gushed, "She is so delicate, and the weather is so very cold. We must take good care of her, on behalf of dear Lord Granville, her betrothed…"

Hunter had to admit that Maria's fame as a great beauty was deserved, but he thought her sister was much more interesting. Nerissa called to his mind images of green, secluded glades, limpid forest pools and the scent of freshly mown grass and crushed mint leaves.

He remembered that rather disappointing visit, as he walked through the park in the crisp early day. It was particularly cold that morning - the frozen ground crackled under his booted feet as he walked, and his breath surrounded his face with a hazy, silvery cloud. The path led him out of a copse of thick trees, and suddenly he saw Nerissa, perched on a fence, writing in a leather bound journal of some kind.

The morning sun, now risen far enough to touch this sheltered spot, painted her with golden highlights, contrasted against the greys and browns of the landscape, with as sure a touch as a Flemish master.

She was totally absorbed in her task and did not see him until he was almost upon her. Some sound of his passage must have penetrated her concentration, for, suddenly, she looked up, startled, gasped, lost her balance and would have tumbled onto the damp, hard ground, had not Hunter, his reflexes honed to a fine edge, caught and held her.

Time froze - he had her in his arms, soft, lissom, vibrant, her deliciously lush, kissable mouth half open in fright, her wonderful eyes wide, a rosy flush on her marvellous high cheekbones. Hunter felt as if something deep in his soul was stirring, some half-forgotten magic, a hopeful wonder he was only dimly aware of. Then, reality reasserted itself, with its rules, shattering the enchantment. Hunter steadied Nerissa and let her go.

"I always seem to scare you, Lady Nerissa." he quipped with a smile.

She smiled in return, an impish smile that reminded him of the ten year old Nerissa, an elfin creature who was always lurking, or trailing in his wake.

"Awkward, am I not, my Lord? I should have played the damsel in distress and feigned a fainting fit – at least that is what my mother would expect me to do", she replied, straightening her pelisse.

Hunter caught her slim little hand in his own.

"It's a good thing I interrupted you - look at your fingers, they're blue with cold."

She briskly took her hand away from his and put on her gloves.

"My tomboy past is coming back to haunt me, my Lord. I used to climb that fence and pretend it was the mainmast of a pirate ship, and I, a daring Pirate, looking for a Spanish galleon to plunder. Ahoy! Ship to starboard, mates!"

Hunter laughed aloud, something he had not done for quite some time.

Sobering, he looked at Nerissa, becoming lost in her mischievous green-gold eyes. There was something so refreshing, so exciting, about this beautiful young woman, who was not trying to attract his attention, or playing the coy maiden or – and he smiled again – the damsel in distress. It was as if she was unaware of her own beauty, unaware of the effect that she had on him (or, he amended, that she likely had on any other man with eyes!).

Unexpectedly at ease with each other, they strolled together, grateful to the inclement weather, which allowed them some time alone, no one the wiser.

~~~~~~~~~~

They met again during the following weeks, always with the same strange mixture of mutual attraction and camaraderie, of shared laughter and untold feelings. They were deeply aware of the impropriety of it, but somehow unable to stop themselves, unable to care about those rules, which seemed so irrelevant, when they were in each other's presence.
~~~~~~~~~~

Hunter would brush his fingers against her smooth cheek, with the excuse of removing a speck of dust, she would daringly straighten his neck-cloth. Nerissa would wait for him, half hidden behind a majestic old beech tree and boo loudly, trying to frighten him. Hunter would encourage her tendency to do unladylike things – he showed her how to skate on the frozen pond using wooden clogs, a trick he had learned of in the Netherlands.

Those winter mornings became a world of their own, separate from the rest of their lives, removed from the rules of society and the expectations of others, in which they learned to know each other and in which their budding friendship strengthened.

Hunter found it unexpectedly easy to tell Nerissa about the war, about his guilt at not having been home when his father had died, about his doubts in his role as a Duke – the role that he had never expected to need to fulfil. Nerissa listened with a sympathetic ear and, when she felt gloom was becoming too pervasive, she made him laugh with her whimsical sense of humour.

Laughing aloud – a practice strongly disapproved of by the straitlaced Lady Augusta Chester – was a rare gift and she loved to share it with Hunter. She loved to be able to smooth his darkening brow, to see his eyes light up, to see a smile turn up his mouth at its corners.

In turn, Nerissa told Hunter about her parents' wish for her to be married as soon as possible, of her own misgivings, of the suitors that Viscount Chester approved – prosy bores, each and every one of them.

"But what can a young lady do, but marry?" she had asked him once.

"Even if one has dreams of her own…" and had suddenly snapped her mouth shut, as if to cut off the words, as if caught on the brink letting a secret slip out.

A secret, Hunter felt, that had to be connected with those strange drawings of hers that he had glimpsed, on their first meeting in the park. Something he had tried to inquire about, only to be thwarted and misled each time.

A girl with dreams of her own. A girl with a mysterious interest that she would not speak about. A girl soon to be married off to somebody not of her choosing. There was nothing unusual in that – quite the expected situation, amongst the *ton*. Hunter did not know why such a normal occurrence should make him feel so uneasy, should weight on his soul like a dark pall. But it did.

Chapter Four

The Season was just beginning when his Grace the Duke of Melton, his family and their retinue arrived in London.

The housekeeper and the butler, who had been dispatched a week before to open up the London house and make it ready, welcomed them on their arrival. The journey had been unexceptional, the road in reasonable condition and the inns comfortable enough.

Charles had planned everything - to the family's satisfaction and to Hunter's vast relief. To be sure, he thought, the forced march from Vitoria to Pamplona, in hot pursuit of the retreating French troops, in some ways paled in comparison to the logistics involved in moving his family from Meltonbrook Chase to London, a scant 140 miles away.

The first days were hectic, with a seemingly incessant stream of tradesmen conferring with Lady Melton and the housekeeper, and with a whirlwind of shopping expeditions to milliners, haberdashers, shoemakers and couturieres.

Strongly backed by Lady Melton, Bulwick succeeded at last in whisking Hunter off to Meyer's of Conduit Street, one of the fashionable men's tailors, and achieving his heart's desire of arranging enough fashionable attire to outfit him to a standard, as the valet put it, suitable for one of the better-looking gentlemen in London.

Hunter had suffered his thick and unruly dark mahogany locks to be cut and styled in a fashionable "a la Brutus" coiffure, but, to Bulwick's consternation, had consistently refused to use a quizzing glass or a cane.

"My good man," he had firmly stated "I'm neither infirm nor in my dotage and my sight is excellent. Please give up bothering me, will you?"

~~~~~~~~

Back in London, Hunter had met again with his friends, a close-knit group of young men with whom he had spent most of his soldiering years.

He had, somewhat to his surprise, missed them terribly whilst at Meltonbrook Chase, and had discovered, to his chagrin, that he had very little in common with either his brother, dear as he was to him, or with Kevin, Lord Chester's son, who had been his best friend before the war.

The war.

Like a scythe, it had cleaved his life into two halves, causing an irrevocable breach.
~~~~~~~~

On one side, there was a carefree young man, driving his curricle at breakneck speed and riding to hounds on his chestnut hunter, given to light flirtation, pranks and bets.

On the other side, there was a sombre gentleman who felt that he did not, really, have a fixed place of his own, who was unsure of his role, saddled with all the honours and obligations inherent in his title and his rank, without any of the training and preparation required to deal with them.

He could share his uneasiness only with his friends. Somehow, they were, in certain ways, more family than his blood relatives were.

Somehow, they had taught him the very meaning of friendship: not some casual, albeit cordial, acquaintance, but somebody upon whom you could blindly rely, somebody who would look out for you, somebody who could understand your feelings without a single word needing to be said, somebody you could tell everything, even your worst weaknesses, faults and mistakes, without being judged or blamed.

They were very different from each other, yet somehow their talents, as a whole, were more than their simple sum.

They were, together, a force to be reckoned with.

Hunter Barrington, Duke of Melton. Charlton Edgeworth, Viscount Pendholm. Lord Barton Seddon. Lord Geoffrey Clarence. Mr Raphael Morton. Gerald Otford, Baron Tillingford.

His Majesty's Hounds, as they had been nicknamed in France and Spain, for their ability to sniff out the enemy's infiltrators, and their most secret plans.

The previous evening they had met, and joked about their rusty social skills.

Charlton had done some wickedly funny impersonations. He had wonderful abilities as a mimic. Abilities which had stood him in good stead during the intelligence forays, which were one of the Hounds' allotted tasks in the field,

His impressions of portly aristocrats squeezed inside creaking corsets, of studiously bored, languid dandies ogling the ladies through bejewelled quizzing glasses and of swaggering Corinthians talking their almost unintelligible sporting cant. They had all laughed until their sides ached, and agreed that they would never ever behave in such a foppish, ridiculous, preposterous way.

"No delicately reared female will spare us a glance… we have to accept the simple fact that we are not good *ton*," Geoffrey had sighed, theatrically.

"Don't tell my mother," Hunter had cut in "she would have me marry whatever girl would have me, bed her and even breed before the Season is over, if that were possible."

"In that precise order?" Barton had queried.

Everybody had laughed. Gerald had arched his eyebrows in supercilious disdain. "The marriage Mart is rather like a fox hunt, you know. We, the eligible bachelors, are the quarry, and the marriageable damsels are the hunters, cheered on by their (and alas, by our) dear Mamas."

"A sobering thought, and one that makes me feel a real sympathy for the poor fox, if it suffers like we do when trying to evade pursuit", Raphael had countered.

It had been a good evening, warm with friendship and shared laughter.

But by now the Season was in full swing and social duties must be met. It would be impossible for them to soon meet again. At the end of the evening, Hunter had donned his greatcoat and beaver hat and gone home, to the townhouse that did not yet feel at all like home, a deep frown creasing his brow.

~~~~~~~~

The whole *ton* agreed that the successful opening event of the Season had been Lord Edmund Wollstonefort, Earl of Granville's wedding to the beauteous Lady Maria Loughbridge.

The bride, a vision of loveliness in her pale ivory gown, had almost floated down the aisle, on her doting Papa's arm, while the besotted groom waited for her. The wedding feast, held at Viscount Chester's townhouse, had been granted the status of a grand squeeze by the leading hostesses, and the bride – with Lady Jersey's permission – had dared to waltz with the groom, followed by the reproving eyes of some of the old fashioned high sticklers. Nobody had noticed the bride's younger sister, a tall, gawky girl with an angular face, dressed in a nondescript, exceedingly modest, pale pink gown (which did not suit her colouring at all...).

~~~~~~~~

Nerissa was with her mother, visiting the *Salon* of the noted French couturiere, Madame Beaumarais, a tiny woman with sparkling, shrewd, birdlike black eyes and profusely crimped blond hair of an improbable shade.

Madame asked Nerissa to turn around slowly, mumbling to herself. She perused some fabric samples and a huge portfolio of illustrations of designs and patterns, while listening to the incessant stream of suggestions made by Lady Chester.

After some time, the couturiere raised her hand and spoke.

"*Assez*! My dear Lady Chester, you would have your daughter dressed like a dowdy country miss. Look at her, *s'il vous plait*. Her colouring is very striking and unusual. She has presence. She has a good body…"

"You are too bold, Madame Beaumarais," Lady Chester replied coldly, while Nerissa listened, taken aback by this evaluation of her assets.

The couturiere shrugged, in a very Gallic fashion.

"Be that as it may. Do it your way, and she will be lucky to marry a country squire. Do it my way, and she will be the rage of this Season."

Lady Chester's eyes shone with an acquisitive glint – Nerissa could tell that she was imagining Nerissa marrying a man as wealthy as Maria's husband.

"Very well, Madame, let us hear your ideas…"

Nerissa was very careful not to look pleased.

Hunter stood in front of the mirror, while Bulwick was painstakingly putting the last, perfecting touches to his cravat, which was tied in an impeccable Mathematical.

He wore the knee length satin breeches, the white silk stockings, the buckled black shoes, the brocade waistcoat and the tight fitting coat required for formal wear and mandatory at Almacks.

"I feel like a dratted fool…" he muttered.

Bulwick gave him a close lipped smile, and shook his head.

"If I may say so, my Lord, I have never before had the good fortune of attending to such a handsome gentleman. You are naturally suited to be dressed to perfection." The valet looked fondly at his master and continued. "You do not need any padding on the shoulders, your calves are elegantly turned yet muscular and you have a very commanding presence…"

"Yes, I look like a foppish effete. Well, if you have quite finished fawning and fussing, I am going. Good evening, Bulwick, and pray do not wait for me. I'm more than able to shrug out of these rags without your help."

Bulwick frowned, but bowed in acquiescence.

"As you wish, my Lord. Good evening."

In the foyer, his sister Alyse looked critically at him and gleefully clapped her hands.

"How handsome you look, Hunter! I declare, you will be surrounded by a full fair of swooning females as soon as you appear at Almacks!"

Hunter smiled. "You look ravishing yourself, little sister. Let us go, it wouldn't do to be late."

It was half past ten when they arrived at Almacks and the rooms were already full. Hunter scanned the crowd for known faces, wondering who of his acquaintance would be in attendance, when suddenly he felt as if his heart had stopped, because before him he beheld the most exquisite creature he had ever seen.

The lady was clad in a forest green gown of a soft, shimmering material, swathing her gracefully. The deceptive simplicity of the cut was not marred by flounces or ruffles and enhanced her delightful shape and flawless complexion. The deep green colour, although very unusual for a younger woman, offset her green gold eyes. Her abundant burnished golden tresses were piled high on her head in a Psyche knot, and braided with green and gold satin ribbons. She looked like a woodland nymph, astoundingly beautiful yet shy, as if the least sudden movement could startle her, and make her disappear into a beam of moonlight.

She was surrounded by a mob of besotted young gentlemen, and Hunter almost had to elbow his way through them to reach her.

The goddess met Hunter's eyes and blushed.

"Good evening, my Lord. How nice to see you. Are you here with your sisters?"

"Lady Nerissa! How are you? I did not expect to see you so soon…"

They exchanged some inconsequential small talk, all the while finding their eyes locked on each other, perhaps rather more so than was polite, their breath caught a little short, each heart beating faster.

"Lady Nerissa, may I ask you to spare a dance for me? Even if I suspect your carnet is already full…"

Nerissa made a show of perusing the booklet. "I am free for the second country dance, if it agrees with you, my Lord."

Hunter bowed slightly, in elegant acknowledgement.

"I look forward to the privilege of dancing with you, Lady Nerissa." As was appropriate, he moved away, to circulate through the room, and socialise.

Nerissa followed him with her eyes. She was elated and frightened at the same time. Hunter in buckskins and jacket was handsome, but Hunter in his evening finery was devastatingly handsome, as the admiring looks from many a young lady clearly showed.

She, herself, did not feel at all the same girl as she was, only a few days before. The new gowns, that Madame Beaumarais had devised for her, had given Nerissa a new assurance, despite her sister's snide remarks about the ugly duckling turning suddenly into a swan.

She had waited, with breathless anticipation, for the moment when chance should provide the opportunity for Hunter to see this new, more confident Nerissa, and she had revelled in his frank admiration.

But what, now? They would meet socially; maybe they would dance together, but it was highly improbable that something more might happen. Both of them had a duty to their families, which a marriage between them could not fulfil.

So, really, it was best that she turn her thoughts elsewhere. Stubbornly, her thoughts refused to be turned.

Nerissa was so absorbed in her musings, she did not realise that the orchestra was striking up with the first bars of the country dance. Hunter appeared in front of her, bowed, took her trembling hand and led her onto the floor.

A sudden hush fell on the ballroom - they were by far the most striking couple in attendance, complementing each other to perfection, moving with effortless grace thorough the intricate steps and turns, bathed in some sort of magic that made those who were looking on hold their breath.

Lady Chester did not miss the alchemy between Nerissa and Hunter and, as soon as the dance ended, was quick to whisk her daughter away.

"I would not have ever believed it, but that Frenchwoman was right and you are on your way to being a great success. Do not be a fool, my daughter, of course, one could not openly scorn the Duke of Melton, but one should not encourage him, do you see? He is by no means as wealthy as many others here. Many gentlemen of impeccable reputation and vast fortunes are vying for your attention - you will have plenty to choose from. Choose wisely."

Nerissa lowered her head and answered as a dutiful daughter should.

"Yes, Mama."

Chapter Five

The season was by now in full swing, a whirlwind of balls, picnics, routs, dinner parties and the like. Hunter and Nerissa met frequently, but never with any chance for private conversation. Both of them remembered, with longing their walks in the park, their conversations, those surreptitious touches, their hands brushing, all the times that they had almost kissed.

The ghost of happiness shimmered in front of them and disappeared, like a puff of smoke. Life was leading them elsewhere, away from each other, away from what now looked like just a foolish and wishful fantasy, a short-lived dream.

Marriage.

Hunter was beginning to hate that word. His mother, who seemed to be finding respite from her bereavement by trying to force him into the parson's mousetrap, was playing the busy matchmaker, much to Hunter's annoyance.

A steady procession of "charming young ladies" were paraded in front of him, in a fashion which Hunter had cynically compared to a cattle fair, during one of his evenings with the Hounds.

"I always wait for my mother to ask them to open their mouth, so that I can inspect their teeth," he had morosely complained. "And musical evenings bore me silly. The last one was a nightmare. I would have rather faced one of old Boney's swordmasters in single combat. "

"I know, Hunter, I was there," Geoffrey had quipped. "That singer – you know, the vast female in pink – sounded rather like a cat caterwauling in a back alley. Absolutely ghastly. And remember, on Friday we shall have to attend to *An Evening with Euterpe* –silly name – at Lady Loynton's."

Hunter smiled. Most of his friends were undergoing the same ordeal as he, and nobody seemed very happy about it.

Well, he had to admit, some of the young ladies he was being introduced to were real beauties, and he was not a monk nor a eunuch. He was as appreciative as the next man of bouncing curls, sparkling eyes, long lashes, rounded arms and swelling bosoms, but, alas, that was that. Past a cursory frisson, an initial appeal, he could not bring himself to really like any of them.

Some of those girls were sweet natured, some were witty, some were attractive, but not a single one of them could make his heart beat faster. Only Nerissa was the least bit engaging - and she was not for him. As had been made clear by the attitude of his mother, and of hers. He needed an heiress, with a substantial dowry, as his mother persistently reminded him.

Nerissa, as Madame Beaumarais had predicted, had become the rage of the season. The latest accolade had been Beau Brummel's approbation and it was becoming fashionable to describe her using one of the scandalous Lord Byron's poems:

She walks in beauty, like the night
Of cloudless climes and starry skies;
And all that's best of dark and bright
Meet in her aspect and her eyes:
Thus mellowed to that tender light
Which heaven to gaudy day denies.

It was rumored that she had already received several marriage offers and had turned down every one, she was seen riding on Rotten Row on her lively mare, often accompanied one of her admirers, but often alone with her groom or with Lady Alyse.

She acquired the fame of being unpredictable and prone to sudden changes of disposition, from friendly to coldly aloof, from dreamy to wickedly witty. The company she kept, the gowns she wore, her mots d'esprit, all became common objects of speculation.

Nobody would have believed that Nerissa was simply bored. After the first weeks of elation at her unexpected social success, the charm of being courted, flattered and singled out began to quickly pale.

The only one whose attentions she really craved did not care for her, this seemed painfully clear. He was the perfect gentleman, but nothing more. Nerissa saw Hunter often enough, but never exchanged more than a few words with him and the ease with which they had talked, laughed and opened their hearts to one another seemed far, far away.

They sometimes danced together, they met during morning visits, they had once watched, together, the fireworks at Vauxhall Gardens, but Hunter had never shown her more than common courtesy, while he showered attentions upon a bevy of fluttering misses, clearly bent on snaring one of the best prizes of the Season. All of them were pretty, all were eligible, all were rich, all had more than willing parents, ready to welcome a Duke with open arms.

And what could she offer but a meagre dowry and hostile parents?

Nerissa sighed. Lady Loynton's *Evening with Euterpe* was more than uncommonly flat and not conductive to uplifting thoughts.

'Give up, Nerissa,' she chided herself. *'And look where you are going, you almost tripped upon Lady Coreley's train. And oh my! Lord Puddleston has seen you!'*

Lord Puddleston was, among her admirers, the only one that she actively disliked. There was something insufferable in his demeanour, a mixture of hauteur and gross familiarity, as if she were nothing but a scullery maid whom he deigned to honour with his regard. Nerissa looked around and saw a half open door. She quickly scuttled in and found herself in the library.

The library! From the beginning of the Season, libraries had been her favourite refuge from bothersome admirers, silly giggling gossips and prying dowagers. Libraries, where she had often discovered interesting books about garden design, thus improving her knowledge. It was remarkable what books various Lords owned.

She looked at the books in this library, and saw, to her excitement and delight, the second tome of Palladio's *I Quattro Libri dell'Architettura* open on a ledger: a most rare and famous text, which she had found quoted in many a treatise, but had never been able to peruse.

Nerissa was soon engrossed, to the exclusion of everything else, in reading the faded pages, written in Italian, a language she knew but imperfectly. Thus, she did not hear the door opening and a soft step on the carpet.

"If it isn't the gorgeous Lady Nerissa hiding away between musty old parchments. What interest could they hold for such as you?"

The lazy drawl and the sneering tone could only belong to the hateful Lord Puddleston, who approached Nerissa with a catlike, menacing ease.

"Reading, are you? Hmmm, let's see... *The second Book of Architecture by Andrea Palladio?*"

He burst out laughing.

"Pretty pictures, are they not? Of course you are looking at the pictures. I refuse to believe that you can actually read, or understand, a treatise on architecture written in Renaissance Italian. You should not fret your pretty little head over these dusty tomes. We could find more congenial ways to wile away the time on this rather tedious evening, you and I..."

Nerissa had realised at once that, by trying to hide from her unwelcome admirer, here, in the library, she had, instead, unwittingly trapped herself.

She was now at risk of becoming entangled in what could well become a very distasteful situation and, while Lord Puddleston was prosing on, she had been looking for an escape route.

And, as luck would have it, found one.

With her practiced eye, attuned to architectural features, she had already noticed that the music room and the library shared the same balcony. With nothing more than a cold look, not even deigning to answer Lord Puddleston's sly innuendo, she turned, quickly unlatched the door, and slipped across the balcony to enter the music room through the doors which had, fortuitously, been opened, to freshen the air after the performance. Moving through the chatting company she sought someone to speak to.

She was safe, this time, but it had been a narrow escape. She had been careless and unconsidered in her actions. In this, her mother was right: it really took very little to mar one's reputation.

~~~~~~~~~

Some days later, Hunter went to Tattersall's with Charles, to choose a new phaeton and horses to put to it. Old Nick, the head groom, had shaken his head and mumbled disapprovingly at his master's lack of a suitable conveyance.

"A gentleman must be seen, must be seen driving, and a fine whip you are for sure, Master Hunter. Your father, bless his soul, had six carriages in his stable. After the accident, your mother went half-mad with grief and ordered everything sold. *"No son of mine will die in a driving accident!*" she cried."
~~~~~~~~~

Nick shook his head again, sadly, as he remembered the Duchess' grief.

"Your brother Charles persuaded her to keep the barouche – for the young ladies, you know - and the travelling coach, but that was that. The phaeton, your curricle, the gig and the chaise had to go."

Apart from the pleasure of visiting Tattersall's and inspecting fine carriages and prime cattle, Hunter was happy to spend some time with his brother. Even living in the same house, their social life was frenzied and left little time for everything else. Also, if truth be known, Hunter had chosen to spend most of his free time with The Hounds, while Charles seemed to be constantly busy with the kind of activities that most young men of the *ton* would scorn – accounts, and plans for rotating crops, reclaiming bogs and improving drainage.

Hunter was beginning to feel a keen interest in the business of being a landed gentleman – he realised that he needed to learn about the way that his estates were managed, but did not want to infringe upon his brother's interests, especially as Charles was managing the estate with foresight and efficiency. He valued those skills, and wanted Charles to know that.

"Well, Hunter, what do you think? These matched red chestnuts look a treat... and they are stallions, not geldings, methinks. They could be put to stud." Charles laughed ruefully and looked sheepishly at his brother.

"I seem not to be able to silence the yeoman in me..."

Hunter laughed in response. "The yeoman in you is a very valuable, very shrewd gentleman. He could teach me a thing or two."

"Would you be interested? I mean, really interested in learning about the land…?"

Hunter looked at his brother, frowning. "Would you mind if I wanted to? Would you help me to learn?"

Charles smiled. "Not in the least. I would be glad. I am, I think, planning to enter the church, you know. I must have a reasonable independence, if I want to marry. And I would be relieved to be able to leave the management of the family estates in your hands. I know that Mother would like to hire a steward, but I am convinced that the landowner must take an interest, lest any hired man fail in his duty and the estate not prosper. I had hoped that you might come to care about these things, but I could not be sure what you might think."

Hunter thumped Charles on the shoulder. "So, my little brother wants to marry! And who is the lucky young lady, may I ask?"

Charles shrugged.

"Call me crazy, she might not want to marry me, now that the whole world is at her feet, but I liked her even when she was bundled up in those awful gowns her mother chose for her. Besides, she has brains, that girl. You know, when Mother was so ill after the accident, old Doctor Stapleford bled her repeatedly, until Nerissa put her foot down and would not let him. He went away in a huff, mumbling about interfering females, but Mother recovered in a thrice."

Of everything his brother had said, Hunter had heard only a single word: Nerissa. Nerissa? Did his brother want to marry Nerissa? **His** Nerissa? Impossible! Inconceivable! Outrageous!

Hunter took a deep breath and tried to get his feelings under control. Why should he be so shocked? His brother wanted to marry Nerissa? There was nothing strange about that – at present, everyone wanted to marry Nerissa, dreamed about Nerissa, lusted after Nerissa.

Besides, how could he prevent his brother from courting Lady Nerissa, their childhood companion, their neighbour, the daughter of one of his father's oldest friends? He had no claim upon her, in fact, he knew very well, as he had only reminded himself last night, that Nerissa was not for him, could never be his. Still the concept did not sit well with him, for some reason.

Now that he knew, he remembered several instances in which he had seen Charles and Nerissa laughing, talking earnestly, their heads together, or riding in the park. Maybe his brother held her esteem, maybe his regard was reciprocated.

Hunter closed his eyes, the brightness of the day suddenly gone.

Pleading fatigue, he left Charles to finish the purchase of the horses, and went back home, changed and spent the evening at White's, playing piquet with Geoffrey and Charlton and rather morosely answering their good natured banter.

Chapter Six

The next morning, Hunter was in a foul temper. He tried, with all his might, to calm down and enumerate the very good reasons why Nerissa and he should not suit.

He had nothing to offer and Nerissa would be better off with somebody who could love her without reservation. The concept of that sort of love terrified him – the pain that he had felt at Beatriz's terrible death, the terrible black emptiness that still waited inside him, surfacing in his dreams, told him that offering anyone love without reservation was a path to the perpetual risk of pain. He could not offer that, could not ever take that risk again. He wanted someone safe, a friend, as a wife, nothing more. And Nerissa deserved more than that, much more. Besides, if he wanted to really improve his estates he had to have a hefty fortune available to him, and the only way to obtain what he needed was to marry an heiress...

Yet, sensible as all of these reasons were, it had been a vain effort.

Nerissa's face, her wonderful slanted eyes, her perfect body enhanced by the bright, bold colours of her gowns, her quick wit, her mysterious passion which resulted in drawings, those dreams that she would not speak about, were ever present in his mind.

And he felt awfully guilty when he considered his brother. He had no right whatsoever to prevent him from courting Nerissa. Charles had cared for his mother and sisters during the difficult time after the accident, had taken over the management of the family estates, had been Nerissa's true friend, well before he, his worthless elder brother, had even taken notice of her. Charles was a steady, responsible young gentleman, capable of deep affection and true commitment. Charles was handsome too, with his raven black hair and keen hazel eyes.

'Look at yourself,' he thought. *'You are a good for nothing bleater. Plagued by your memories, afraid to love again, unable to settle down and do something worthwhile. It would have been better not to sell your commission, to leave Charles to manage your estates and to turn into a hoary old veteran. Admit it, Nerissa deserves far more than the little you can offer her.'*

~~~~~~~~

Lady Chester beamed at her younger daughter, an event almost unheard of, before that fateful Season.

They were seated in the parlour, taking tea, and discussing the social whirl. It was not a conversation that Nerissa cared for, but she had little choice. Her mother could conceive of no more fascinating topic.
~~~~~~~~

"Well, now, my darling, I think that the Earl of Langley is going to drop the question soon. He is a very eligible young gentleman, well-mannered, obliging, attentive and handsome. His reputation is immaculate, he is not a gambler and he does not associate with disreputable acquaintances. Your father tells me his estates are very well managed and unencumbered, his townhouse is in very good taste and his sister is a delightful girl, spirited but sweet natured. Not that you will have to worry about her, she will probably marry in a few months. Lord Ackland seems quite taken with her."

Lady Chester looked speculatively at Nerissa, who was gazing out of the window with unfocused eyes.

"I do hope, Nerissa," she said, with some asperity "that you are not thinking of marrying young Lord Charles Barrington. I know you are fond of him and he is a really nice gentleman, but you can do much better than a younger son, soon to become a clergyman, if I heard Lady Melton correctly. He may currently be Viscount Wareham, as the Duke's heir, but that title will pass to the Duke's son, once he has one, and Lord Charles will be a nobody clergyman. Last year I would have been more than happy for such an alliance, but now..." and she let her voice trail off.

"Do not worry, Mama" answered Nerissa. "I like Lord Charles, but only as a long-time friend, and so I told him. I did not want him to cherish unfounded hopes on my behalf. I am too fond of him to play ducks and drakes with his feelings."

Lady Chester released a sigh of relief at these words, wondering, once again, what magic had transformed her hoydenish younger daughter into this sensible, vibrantly attractive young woman.

"Very good, my dear. I can see that you are a sensible young woman. Now, we have received an invitation for a house party, to be held next week at Lord and Lady Stanmore's country house. It is only a few miles from London, and Lady Bayford has told me that they have recently redone their gardens, in the most delightful fashion. We will attend. You will, of course, need some new gowns and suitable jewellery to go with them. I am sure that Madame Beaumarais will think of something flattering."

Well, Nerissa thought, at least she would be able to have a look at those new gardens. And no more trips into the library, however much she may wish to discover what books her hosts may have! After the near disaster at Lady Loynton's *"Evening with Euterpe"*, she was set on behaving with unimpeachable manners.

~~~~~~~~

"Is it really necessary that we attend, Mother?" Hunter asked in an aggrieved tone. "It really sounds a dead bore. Besides, Lord and Lady Stanmore are not my favourite kind of people. He can speak of nothing but hounds, horses, rifles and game and she is a malicious gossip with a mean attitude."

Lady Melton sighed. "I wish you were less blunt in your speech, Hunter. Speaking one's mind is all well and good, I am sure, in the military, but amongst the *ton* a little tact never comes amiss. One should always avoid giving unnecessary offense or..." She coughed delicately.

Hunter looked at his mother, his eyes dancing with merriment. "Or acting like a sanctimonious prig?"
~~~~~~~~

Lady Melton smiled.

"I would not have put it in such a straightforward manner, but yes, that is the gist of what I meant. Besides, your sisters yearn to go. I believe Alyse nurses a tendre for Lord Uppingham and I would like your opinion of the gentleman. He seems unobjectionable, but…"

"What are you afraid of, Mother dear? Unsavoury acquaintances? Gambling debts? Bits o'muslin hidden away in side streets? A despicable tendency to be foxed at ten o'clock in the morning? A bevy of maiden aunts?"

Charles, who was coming into the drawing room, laughed heartily and Lady Melton blushed.

"You know, Hunter, sometimes I despair of you. These are topics wholly unsuitable for a lady's contemplation."

Hunter smiled.

"Do not fret, Mother, I will investigate. And I will come with you to this insipid house party. It would not be seemly for you and the girls to go alone, without a responsible and sedate male presence."

And with that, Hunter left the room, pretending not to hear Charles' muffled guffaw.

Chapter Seven

A week later, Hunter was regretting his decision. The house party was proving more than uncommonly flat, he sorely missed the Hounds, none of whom had been invited, and the renewed onslaught of marriageable young Ladies, with their hovering mamas, was beginning to grate on his nerves. The way that they looked at him made him develop a sudden sympathy for the horses on show at Tattersall's.

Adding to his discomfort, Nerissa was there, always surrounded by both calf eyed young gentlemen and knowing, jaded rakes, all vying for her attention.

She sparkled, like the diamond of the first water that she was - she flirted, she laughed, she danced and she seemed dusted with some magic powder that made everybody fall under her enchantment.

Lost in his thoughts, Hunter did not realise that his mother was approaching, towing behind her one of her favourite 'suitable young ladies', Lady Phoebe Burnside.

Hunter thought she was a singularly silly girl and, even if she was quite pretty, Hunter feared she would grow to resemble her mother, a wilting lily of indeterminate age, clad in layer upon layer of pale gauze, which gave her a disquietingly ghostly appearance.

"Hunter!" trilled Lady Melton.

"What are you doing here, brooding in this dark corner? Come over to the drawing room, we have prevailed upon Lady Phoebe to sing for us. She has a wonderful voice and she plays the pianoforte with such a delicate touch…"

Lady Phoebe smiled at the handsome Duke, looked at him from half lowered lashes and put a tremulous hand on his sleeve.

"Please, my Lord, I set great store by your opinion. Your lady Mother has told me that you had the great good fortune to listen to Anna Milder-Hauptmann, the famous soprano singer, during her tournèe in London, before the war. I do not presume to compare with her, of course, but if you could listen to me and tell me what you think…"

Short of being rude, there was no way that Hunter could decline the dubious honour which Lady Phoebe had bestowed upon him. Thus, he bowed and followed the ladies into the drawing room.

~~~~~~~~~

Meanwhile, Nerissa was trying to get rid of one of her admirers, Lord Peter Featherstone, who, if one was to believe the current on dits, was soon to be Marquess of Glenfield.
~~~~~~~~~

Nerissa's father liked him quite well, and did not object to his paying court to his daughter.

"Good family," Lord Chester had stated, "good blood. His father is almost booked, poor soul. Wasting sickness. Young Peter will soon be Marquess. His uncle Edward is a bishop, his aunt married the Earl of Balfield, a Scotsman. No siblings, which is well, because Lord Featherstone squandered quite a bit of blunt while sowing wild oats. Well, young men will be young men..."

"My dear sir," her mother had objected, "I do believe Lord Langley would be a more suitable choice. Anyway, there is still time, the Season has not ended yet. Perhaps some better opportunity will turn up. Nerissa is all the rage, you know."

~~~~~~~~

'I really do wish' Nerissa thought *'that my parents would not speak about my marriage as if I were not there. After all, it's me they are bickering about...'*

"A penny for your thoughts..."

Lord Peter Featherstone's voice interrupted her reverie and Nerissa shot him a brilliant smile.

"Nothing of import, my lord. I was thinking of something that my parents told me."

Lord Peter looked at Nerissa. She was a beauty, no doubt about it. Accomplished, pleasing and not an empty-headed ninny, either.

She would make a superb marchioness.
~~~~~~~~

Her dowry was not large, but it was sufficient to appease at least the best part of his debtors. Some vowels of his were in the hands of seedy gentlemen whose main trait was not forbearance.

Lady Nerissa seemed his best hope for a rapid cash infusion, in a woman that he would not be at all unhappy to have in his bed. He had to become betrothed to her soon, lest some more eligible beau should snatch her away. In that instant, a bold plan formed in his mind and he resolved to act upon it straightaway.

~~~~~~~~~

The song had ended, to courteous applause, and Lady Phoebe smiled coyly, curtsied and shot a wishful look at Hunter. She was set on becoming Lady Melton before the Season ended. This was her second Season and, if it ended without anybody asking her to marry them, she would end on the shelf, an old maid of no import.

She yearned to become a Duchess, a leader of fashion, a recognised power amongst the *ton*, but beyond that, she must admit it to herself - Lord Melton turned her knees to jelly.

Up to now, all of her ploys had been unsuccessful - she had failed to catch his attention. Lady Phoebe ground her teeth. It was, she decided, the fault of that hateful Lady Nerissa, preening around in her vulgar gowns. What proper young lady had ever dared to wear burgundy, midnight blue, crimson, emerald green or coral red? Of course nobody could fail to notice her.
~~~~~~~~~

'Well, my lord Duke,' she told herself, *'we shall see. I will not allow you to disregard me. I may play the silly fool, but I'm more than a match for you.'*

~~~~~~~~

Nerissa was sitting on a chair, fanning herself, while Lord Featherstone hovered attentively, offering her a glass of lemonade.

"It is rather stifling inside, isn't it? It seems that half the guests share my opinion, and have made themselves scarce. Have you seen the gardens, Lady Nerissa? Lady Stanmore had them recently redesigned. What say you – shall we stroll a bit and have a look at them? It will be a relief from this overheated room…"

Nerissa hesitated. She did not think it was *comme il faut* to take a turn in the gardens with a gentleman, even if it was true that lots of people were already there.

She sighed, thinking of Hunter and their escapades, wandering the woods and fields of their country homes. It seemed like an impossible dream, so long ago, and so unreachable now. In truth, she also yearned for some fresh air, because the weather had been foggy and wet these last few days and it had been impossible to stay outside for very long.

Lord Featherstone pressed on - "We shall be in full view all of the time and, anyway, rules are not so strict at house parties. Look, Lady Nerissa! There is even a full moon! Think what fun we shall have! Let's go!"
~~~~~~~~

So saying, he took Nerissa by the hand, propelling her across the terrace, and down the stairway leading to the gardens, before she had time to frame a courteous refusal.

~~~~~~~~

Prompted by a darkling look from his mother, Hunter had escorted Lady Phoebe to a window seat and was listening to her inconsequential chit-chat. She was delicately sipping cold lemonade and looking at him with wide, slightly vacant eyes.

"Look, Your Grace, how romantic! Lady Stanmore insisted on having a medieval ruin in her garden and tonight the full moon is rising behind it. Is it not like a fairy tale? One could imagine the Little Folk dancing in a glade and Queen Titania, with a flower crown... My Lord, would it really be so naughty if we were to go for a stroll? It would please me to no end..."

Hunter looked around, feeling a sudden wave of fatigue wash over him. The ladies in their elegant gowns, jewels sparkling at their throats and wrists, the gentlemen in their formal attire, the gossiping matrons: everything seemed meaningless, empty, and ephemeral. Lady Phoebe was looking expectantly at him. It was clear that she wanted to go out, but had hesitated to ask. He considered the idea. *'Why not?'* he thought. At least it would be a respite from the stuffy, overcrowded room.

He smiled

"Could I have the honour of escorting you for a short walk in the gardens, Lady Phoebe?"

She smiled graciously.
~~~~~~~~

"Gladly, my Lord."

Whilst she spoke demurely, inside, she was exulting - she had succeeded, her ruse had worked. Now, for the final strike! An almost shifty, covetous look in her eyes, she went down the staircase, her hand lightly reposing on Hunter's arm.

~~~~~~~~

"What do you think of Lady Stanmore's medieval ruin, Lady Nerissa?"

"An eyesore" she answered without thinking.

Lord Peter laughed.

"You do have taste, Lady Nerissa. You are not in the least conventional, you know. Conversing with you is a rare pleasure."

Turning her towards him, he put his hands on her shoulders.

"And your beauty is enough to make a man crazed..."

His arm encircled her waist, pulling her against him and he kissed her hard. Nerissa tried to free herself, but her struggle was in vain. Lord Peter held her in an iron grip. She let out a muffled cry of outrage at that cavalier treatment, but he was not to be denied.

~~~~~~~~

He had wandered with Lady Phoebe, aimlessly, for a while, when Hunter realised that there was nobody anywhere near them and began to feel distinctly uneasy.

"We really should return, Lady Phoebe. Our absence could be noticed…"

"Let's go a bit further, my lord." she cajoled, pouting. "The ruin is just a short way ahead, and I do so wish to see it close up! I am sure that nothing untoward could befall me in your company. Besides, you are a war hero, are you not? You would protect me against any evildoer, would you not?"

In that moment Hunter perceived a movement, just beyond the corner of the ruin which they were approaching, saw a flash of burgundy silk, and suddenly remembered that Nerissa was wearing a burgundy gown that evening. Upon hearing a muffled sound, which was alarming like a squeal of protest, he started to run, unintentionally towing behind him the bewildered Lady Phoebe, who clung to his arm like a limpet.

He turned the corner of the artfully constructed ruin, and beheld an unknown blackguard, who was holding a struggling Nerissa and trying to silence her with a kiss. It was like some sort of awful déjà vu, a re-enactment of his nightmares. Only, this time, it was not Beatriz, but Nerissa, fighting a man who was attempting to take advantage of her. And in was not a dream, but the harsh reality.

"Let her go, you scoundrel!" Hunter roared, barely arresting his forward motion before colliding with the struggling couple. He caught Nerissa's hand, and pulled her hard towards him, twisting her out of Lord Peter's clutches.

Hunter had moved at lightning speed and, in so doing, had unbalanced Lady Phoebe, who had still been clinging to his arm with grim determination. The twist that freed Nerissa strained the final limits of Lady Phoebe's balance.

Unable to help herself, she let go of his arm and was thrown forward, directly towards Lord Peter.

Lord Peter, flabbergasted at the sudden wrenching disappearance of the woman in his arms, and unbalanced himself by her removal, had stumbled forward, promptly colliding with Lady Phoebe. With an automatic reflex, he tried to prevent Lady Phoebe from falling and found, in a strange juxtaposition of circumstances, that he was holding her in his arms.

Meanwhile Hunter, stumbling backwards from the force of Nerissa's arrival in his arms, to end leaning against the wall of the artful ruin, found himself still holding her, as she collapsed against him, faint with relief at her unexpected deliverance from peril.

"You play the gallant knight very well, my Lord", she whispered.

"And you make a very fetching damsel in distress," he replied.

He knew that he had to let her go, to restore her to balance and to a less dishevelled state, but somehow he could not. She was leaning into his strength with artless abandon, as if she had finally found her place.

In that precise moment, an older couple appeared, walking sedately around the bend in the path - none other than their hosts, Lord and Lady Stanmore. It took only an instant for Lady Stanmore to take in the most unseemly scene. Lady Phoebe, panting and dishevelled, in the arms of Lord Peter Featherstone and Lady Nerissa, locked with His Grace of Melton in what appeared to be a steamy embrace.

Eyes shining as she took in every aspect of the scene before her, obviously to memorise the juicy details for further reference and embroidery of description, she took a deep breath before she spoke.

"Well, well, if we did not stumble upon a whole dovecote of love birds… I did not expect that my new garden would prove quite so conductive to dalliance… Ladies and gentlemen, please compose yourselves and follow us back to the house, immediately. I will not have my house party disgraced by your wanton behaviour. I do believe that your parents should be informed at once and that appropriate action needs to be taken." There was no mistaking her meaning, not the determined expression in her eye.

Having delivered her speech, Lady Stanmore marched toward the house, followed by a subdued Nerissa, a brooding Hunter, a black browed Lord Peter and a wailing Lady Phoebe.

Within a few minutes of their return, the whole drawing room was buzzing with rumours. Behind their fans the ladies exchanged titbits of what promised to become the scandal of the Season, involving, moreover, the much sought after Lady Nerissa.

"Half naked, Lady Stanmore told me…"

"A secret assignation, imagine that!"

"Who knows how long they may have been carrying on…"

"Maybe not only kissing, my dear…"

"Alone, in the garden, at night…"

"I would never have thought…"

"Such nice young ladies…"

"Beware of still waters…"

In a dark corner, Lady Phoebe was crying her heart out, while her mother patted her head and tried to soothe her.

"Worse luck, my daughter, but you landed a title anyway. A Marchioness is not a Duchess, true, but it is the next best thing. And do not concern yourself so. Your dear Papa shall make the Marquess marry you, do not doubt it…"

Suddenly, everybody stopped talking. A very pale Duke of Melton walked toward Lord Chester, bowed before him, and spoke, the words ringing clear and true in the silent room.

"My lord, may I ask you to do me the great honour of granting me your daughter's hand in marriage?"

Lord Chester regarded him with an icy stare. It was clear that His Grace of Melton's suit was not relished, but that it would be accepted to ensure the prevention of a very disagreeable scandal.

"You have my permission to marry my daughter Nerissa, my lord Duke. Please meet me the day after tomorrow to go through the formal agreement. I have a few things to discuss with you and you would do well to pay close attention." Then he addressed his wife.

"Madam, tomorrow we return to London. You shall have plenty to do, if we are to arrange Nerissa's marriage before the Season ends."

Chapter Eight

Hunter walked out of Lord Chester's study in a much-improved frame of mind. He had been able to reassure his father-in-law-to-be about himself. It had been hard for him to talk about the war and about His Majesty's Hounds and their role, as much of it as he was at liberty to discuss, but he had felt the need to make Lord Chester understand that he, Hunter Barrington, Duke of Melton, was not a wild and dissipated boy anymore.

As luck would have it, Lord Wilfred Dartworth, former leader of the Hounds, whose role Hunter had taken on after his untimely death, happened to have been one of Lord Chester's friends and this had done much toward easing their relationship.

Hunter had frankly explained the freak accident in Lady Stanmore's garden, but assured Lord Chester of his willingness to marry Nerissa, whom he held in high regard.

His marriage had come about in a strange enough manner - he wanted to start his wedded life on good terms with his soon-to-be wife's parents.

To this purpose, he had asked to speak with Lady Chester as well, and found her already well disposed toward him. Lady Chester was, in the end, pragmatic – if her daughter was to wed in such circumstance, far better it be to a Duke, than to a less reputable man, or one of lesser rank.

Hunter was worldly enough to see, perfectly well, that a Duke was a Duke, however tarnished his reputation. The wily Lady Phoebe had valued his title enough, it seemed, to stage an elaborate ruse to try to force him into marriage. Only the accident of them arriving in the same place as Lord Peter and Lady Nerissa had prevented it from being he who was found with Lady Phoebe in his arms. Hunter was profoundly grateful for the way things had turned out.

Now he had to speak with Nerissa, the most difficult task of all. He had tried, for all of the previous day and night, to unravel the knot of his feelings, but the results of his efforts had been poor. He was still not clear, in his own mind, of exactly what his feelings were. He knew that he was strongly attracted to her, and he was also aware of his deep unease when he saw her with other men.

'Deep unease!' he told himself *'You would do well to get rid of the niceties, cease mincing words, and call it by its name, jealousy, and be done with it…'*

An unwanted image intruded on his mind. Nerissa as he had seen her two days ago, scared and trembling in his arms, but still spirited enough to joke about her predicament. No, he could not regret the blind fate that had forced his hand -overall, he could not say that he was unhappy. He wondered, though, about Nerissa's feelings – could she be happy with him?

He would give her as much of himself as he could, and, with luck, they would at least be able to resume the kind of friendship they had felt, for that magical time before they had gone to London, when they had walked and talked in the silence of the winter fields and woods.

More than this, he did not dare to hope for.

He stood a full minute in front of the morning room door, then braced himself and asked the footman to announce him.

~~~~~~~~

Nerissa knew that Hunter was closeted with her father and could not help but be anxious about it.

She knew that Lord Chester had little use for Hunter, whom he still saw as the mischievous boy he remembered, given to practical jokes and outrageous pranks, not as the head of his family.

She had deep misgivings about this marriage, forced upon both of them by the failed scheming of others. Even if she admitted to being in love with Hunter, she did not think her feelings were reciprocated.

And yet, recalling the events of that fateful evening, she realised that she had never felt as protected, as whole, as alive as she had felt while Hunter held her, after having rescued her from the loathsome Lord Peter's clutches.

'If Lord Peter's plan had succeeded, I would be marrying him.' she thought, shivering.

Her mother had thoroughly catechised her before her betrothed's visit.
~~~~~~~~

"His Grace of Melton's prompt request for your hand in marriage has avoided a most unsavoury scandal, but now you must act with utmost caution. I know, it was not your fault, Lord Peter Featherstone proved to be an out and out rascal and Lady Phoebe, the little viper, is very welcome to have him, and to keep him if she can. But now we must deal with Lord Melton, who has revealed himself to be a true gentleman. He must not think you forward or fast. You must be reserved, modest, grateful but just a bit reluctant, do you understand?"

"Yes, Mama. Maybe it would be more honest if I refused him. I do not want him to think that I sought to trap him."

Lady Chester had shot her daughter an outraged look.

"Do not even think about it, my daughter. I will not have my family disgraced. If not of yourself, think of your sister. You would not want her to be besmirched by a scandal which is none of her doing, would you?"

"No, Mama, of course not. I will wed him."

"Good. Now try to relax. I will send a maid with some hot tea to revive you. And pinch your cheeks, you are too pale."

Lady Chester had left, in a swirl of peach sarsenet, while Nerissa sipped pensively at her tea and tried to divert her mind by leafing through a much coveted and newly acquired tome on her favourite subject, garden design.

She was deeply absorbed in Humphry Repton's *Fragments on the Theory and Practice of Landscape Gardening,* when the footman knocked at the door and announced:

"His Grace the Duke of Melton to see you, my Lady."

She composed herself, stood up, straightened her shoulders and took a deep steadying breath. Absentmindedly, thinking only of Hunter, and what they might say to each other, she left her book open on the chaise where she had been sitting.

"Please tell his Grace to come in, Fenton."

Hunter stood transfixed, looking at Nerissa. She was standing in front of the window, framed by rich brocade curtains, clad in a morning gown of periwinkle blue muslin, a paisley shawl on her arms, a necklace of freshwater pearls and lapis lazuli around her throat.

A sunbeam bathed her in a golden halo, enhancing the colour of every strand of her hair, lighting her perfect skin, turning her into a vision of breath-taking loveliness.

Nerissa smiled.

"Welcome, Your Grace, please, be seated. Fenton, have some refreshment brought."

Hunter sat down on the indicated chaise, and could not fail to notice the open book next to him, a mint new copy of the rather controversial *Fragments on the Theory and Practice of Landscape Gardening,* showing an exquisitely detailed plan for a formal garden, complete with an arboretum of exotic trees, a grotto with a rock garden and a monk's garden.

Suddenly, the drawings he had seen, falling from Nerissa's portfolio that very first day in the woods, took on a completely different significance.

He remembered how he had been agreeably surprised by the improvement in Viscount Chester's park. He realised in that instant, that Nerissa herself must have had a hand in planning them.

Her talent stunned him, and, thinking back to Lady Stanmore's much-vaunted new garden, he felt that Nerissa's work, as demonstrated by the garden's here, was much more original and innovative.

If this was Nerissa's secret, he could not blame her for hiding it.

Landscape and garden design, and architecture, were not counted among approved occupations for young ladies. It seemed so typical of Nerissa, that the thing she cared deeply about should be a thing that she 'shouldn't do'. The thought brought a wry smile to his face. These were the things that he most liked about her – the things that made her herself.

Still, seeing her somewhat serious face, he decided not to speak about it yet - he would wait for her to trust him enough to confide in him.

~~~~~~~~~

Nerissa looked at Hunter, who, somehow, managed to look more handsome and wonderful than ever – which was rather an achievement, after a long and serious conversation with her father!

He seemed unsure, and the silence was dragging on, as they simply looked at each other.
~~~~~~~~~

The silence needed to be broken – suddenly, she decided to speak her mind. This was one of the most important events in her life and she did not intend to play the coy maiden.

"My lord Duke, I'm deeply grateful to you - you saved me from a very difficult situation. I was caught, if you will forgive my saying so, between a rock and a hard place. Had you not intervened, I would have been obliged to marry that knave. You already had my friendship, now you have my undying gratitude as well. I..." she blushed, "I am honoured to be your bride, but you must tell me truly - is this prospect, I mean, marrying me, distasteful to you?"

~~~~~~~~

Hunter looked at Nerissa, not quite believing what he had heard. Did she fear to be rejected? Did she think herself not good enough for him?

In a flash, he saw her again, valiantly struggling to free herself from Lord Peter Featherstone's unrequested advances, a sylph fighting an ogre, and felt an overwhelming desire to hold her, to kiss her, to bury his hands in her marvellous silken hair, to caress her, to love her. The intensity of it shocked him – it was by far the strongest desire that he had ever felt.

She was watching him, in that trusting, open way she had, the way that, he realised, she saved for him, had done so since those first conversations in the icy woods. She was waiting for his answer, trusting him to be honest with her. The intensity of his desire for her redoubled, and he forced it back – he had to find the words, now, to reassure her.
~~~~~~~~

It had lasted just an instant, that rush of desire, of care, before Hunter had schooled his expression back to a courteous interest, but his eyes had lit up with the intensity and passion of his feelings for her - and Nerissa had seen it.

Before he even spoke, a warm glow surrounded her – that look in his eyes had told her all that she needed to know.

Chapter Nine

True to his word, Hunter came to collect Nerissa the next morning, for the promised ride in Hyde Park. She was ready and waiting for him in the hall, with her smiling mother at her side.

"Good morning, Your Grace. Here is my Nerissa, all ready - take good care of her."

"I will, my lady. The weather is ideal for a drive, sunny and pleasantly warm, now that the winter is leaving us."

"Don't forget your parasol, Nerissa." Lady Melton fretted, "You would not want your complexion to be an unseemly shade of tan, like a peasant girl, on your wedding day!"

"Don't worry, mother, I have it here." She kissed her mother's cheek and followed Hunter from the house.

The footman handed Nerissa into the high perch phaeton, drawn by a pair of obviously quality frisky red chestnuts, and they were off at a brisk pace.

They made a stunning couple and many a head turned to look at them.

Nerissa looked quite lovely in a coral pink and coral red silken striped carriage dress, complemented by a coral pink bonnet trimmed with cream feathers and coral red ribbons. Madame Beaumarais had outdone herself, again.

Hunter looked every inch the distinguished gentleman, with his brocade waistcoat, midnight blue coat, tight pantaloons and shining Hessian boots.

After a good night's sleep, for once free from nightmares, that morning he felt happier and more carefree than he had for a long time. He felt invigorated by the fresh morning air, unaccountably excited by Nerissa sitting at his side and by the prospect of, again, driving a fast, sporting carriage. It was as if the reckless boy he had been was alive again, on that spring morning, taunting him to some wild dare.

Nerissa had been driving in the park quite often, but never in such a modish carriage, or with such an accomplished and handsome driver. She revelled in the sense of freedom, in the fresh country smells of the park and in Hunter's presence so near her.

The narrow seat compelled them to touch often and, through the thin fabric of her gown, Nerissa could feel Hunter's hard muscled thigh pressing against hers. It was a strangely intimate contact, which unsettled her more than she cared to admit.

She tried to take refuge in conversation, but meanwhile they had reached Rotten Row and Hunter was putting the chestnuts through their paces, his concentration on them for the moment.

The wildness encouraged Hunter to take the horses rather faster, at least for a moment, than was generally regarded as suitable for the Park, and the delight in Nerissa's eyes made him glad that he did. The spirited horses responded well and the phaeton picked up speed, swaying from side to side on its spring suspension and making them bump into each other often.

More than once Hunter kept her from unbalancing by encircling her waist with one arm. More than once Nerissa found herself leaning against him, the ribbons of her bonnet flying wildly behind her.

They rode on, laughing, touching, exhilarated by their nearness, by speed, by a heady feeling of daring and freedom.

After a while Hunter reined in and the horses slowed down to a more sedate pace. They looked at each other, a high colour whipped into their cheeks by the wind, their eyes sparkling, both slightly panting and dishevelled. A sudden feeling of rightness, of belonging with each other, overcame them and left them speechless.

They rode back in silence, knowing that something wonderful had happened, but unwilling to name it yet.

Life became hectic in the weeks preceding their marriage - both Lady Melton and Lady Chester had insisted on a sumptuous marriage, with all of the *ton* in attendance.

Both Nerissa and Hunter had repeatedly stated that they did not care for such an ostentatious affair, but to no avail - their mothers presented a common front and vetoed their pleas.

"You must understand, my dear boy," Lady Melton had said to her son, with the slightly cajoling tone one might use with a person of slightly slow comprehension, "that a fashionable marriage is unavoidable, given the…er…strange circumstances of your betrothal. We must dispel any doubt that this is a love match, that you and Nerissa had a long-time understanding and that only the fear of her father's displeasure had prevented you from asking for her hand earlier. Do you see?"

Yes, he saw, even if it did not please either him or Nerissa.

They visited with each other every day, and she often complained to him of the endless arrangements.

"If I see another guest list I'll scream. If I have to endure another pointless argument about whether to invite or not to invite Lord Something or Lady Whatever or whether Second-Cousin-Thrice-Removed Sir Goodsort will or will not be offended if he does or does not receive an invitation card…"

Hunter laughed, rather mirthlessly, sharing her frustration.

"I know. Had I only imagined all this completely meaningless fuss, I would have eloped with you and married you over the anvil in Gretna Green."

Nerissa giggled.

"And gladly would I have come with you. Does one really marry over an anvil? I am very curious. Perhaps we are still in time to find out…"

Hunter shook his head glumly.

"Do not tempt me, my affianced bride. I could pick you up willy-nilly, abduct you and drive you up to Scotland in a thrice."

Nerissa looked at Hunter with a wicked gleam in her eyes.

"Would it be an abduction, I wonder?"

Hunter groaned.

"Insufferable brat. I do believe you have not changed a whit since you were a pesky ten-year-old."

They laughed together and the boring details of their marriage faded away in their shared amusement.

They grew closer each day, the subtle ties of a shared childhood, and the weeks of conversation after his return from the war, subtly and unconsciously changing into something else, into a more complex, and somehow baffling relationship.

Their mutual attraction played a part as well, and, as constricted as they were by social convention, and by the educated compulsion to behave properly, the urge to touch, to be near, to kiss was always present, if never indulged.

Meanwhile, they were involved in the whirlwind of their social life with their new status as betrothed, which granted them a degree of freedom that they had not previously enjoyed.

There were picnics and balls, there were outings and strolls - as both Nerissa and Hunter were not late risers, unlike most of the *ton*, there were early morning rides in Hyde Park, which became their favourite time of the day for being together.

Nerissa had to undergo the seemingly never ending fittings of her wedding gown – which also involved tolerating the constant bickering, between Madame Beaumarais and her mother, about how her gown should be fashioned.

"Do you want your daughter to look like a meringue? Like a meringue trimmed with whipped cream?" the Frenchwoman would argue.

"No, I do not, but neither do I want her to look like a nun. Simple is all well and right, but too simple, no, it is not! This is a marriage, not a penitential pilgrimage!" Lady Chester would shoot back.

During these clashes between the two strong willed women, neither used to being naysaid, Nerissa did not even try to participate in the discussion. She simply allowed it to wash over her, allowed herself to be poked and prodded, turned this way and that, as they wished.

She really did not care about her appearance, as long as she knew that she would be marrying Hunter.

It all seemed dreamlike, a whirlwind of activity which swept her along, with or without her cooperation. She could not yet believe that she was really going to marry him, even if through a serendipitous cause.

'What if it is only a dream?' she thought. *'What if he changes his mind?'*

On a sunny afternoon, after a meeting with the florist to plan the ballroom decorations, Nerissa was sipping a cold drink of mint and lemon juice, when the footman announced Hunter's visit.

Nerissa was so glad to see him that she had to restrain herself from running to him. It was quite a challenge to wait for him to come into the room, for her to stay primly sitting on the sofa.

They talked together about their mutual friends, about the journey to the Lake District that they were planning to make after their marriage, and Nerissa gave him a humorous account of her plight, as a victim of both her mother and Madame Beaumarais.

"Poor Nerissa," laughed Hunter "A dove caught in the cruel talons of two hawks… It is a blessing for us gentlemen to have fewer choices to make about our attire."

"You look very elegant in your city clothes, but I liked you also in your buckskins and riding boots."

Smiling, Hunter caught her hands in his.

"Mmmmh, so you liked me! You never told me that!"

She smiled.

"How improper of me, should I have done so. I should not be so forward, my mother told me so."

Hunter kissed her hands and, raising his eyes, he looked at her full, laughing mouth and could not resist. He circled her waist with his arm, lowered his head to meet hers, and kissed her.

He had meant it to be a chaste, almost brotherly kiss, but, as soon as he felt the petal soft texture of her sweet lips, he was lost. The kiss deepened, became passionate, alive with an almost primal urgency. Nerissa, startled at first, then did not hesitate to reciprocate - with a degree of abandon that delighted Hunter.

Surprised, Nerissa wondered how it could be possible for the same act to be repugnant or wonderful when performed by two different men.

She still vividly remembered the disgust and the outrage she had felt, when Lord Peter had tried to kiss her. Why then, did she enjoy so much being kissed by Hunter, and wish for the kiss never to stop? Before rational thought forsook her, a little voice in her head whispered: *'because you love him, you ninny.'*

The kiss seemed to last only a second, and yet forever, but eventually they broke apart, panting and bewildered by the naked intensity of the emotion they had shared. Hunter gave her a tentative smile.

"I should apologise for my behaviour, but the truth is that I have longed to kiss you since that day in your park, when you almost fell down from the fence."

"And I wish you had. After all, a kiss is the just guerdon a brave knight has a right to claim for rescuing a damsel in distress."

Hunter laughed outright.

"I must remind you, then, my belle dame sans merci, that I rescued you twice."

"Claim your prize, then, mon brave."

Hunter looked at her askance.

"Provoke me at your risk. I plan to claim my full prize, ma cherie, but not now..."

Nerissa blushed furiously but bravely met his eyes.

"It will never be too soon."

They clasped hands and stood looking at each other, shaken by the strength of their feelings.

Chapter Ten

Hunter spent a troubled night, torn between hope and fear, anticipation and anxiety. He relived, over and over the previous afternoon's events, and could not regret them.

He had acted on impulse, without restraint, it was true, but he had been amply rewarded by Nerissa's unabashed and yet innocent enthusiasm.

Could he dare to hope? Was there a future of happiness for him? Did he deserve to be happy? Had he not forfeited his right to love again by not being able to protect Beatriz from a horrible death? Then, when dawn was already brightening the horizon, he finally fell asleep.

In his dream, he was walking along a country lane, under an indigo twilight sky. A light breeze was blowing, sweet with scents of honeysuckle and wild roses.

A faint pink hue was still visible in the west and a soft, glowing mist extended its silver ribbons between the trees.

The beauty of the peaceful landscape was like a balm for Hunter's battered soul, soothing his anxiety, assuaging his fears.

Suddenly, out of the mist, a feminine figure appeared.

She was swathed in layers and layers of incorporeal veils, somehow shaped like vast, shimmering wings, gathered around an inner core of splendour. She emanated a feeling of peace and of ineffable joy.

Hunter stopped, in awe of the mysterious being, and, when she was near enough for him to see her face, he was stunned to discover that she was none other than Beatriz, his long mourned love.

Beatriz, not as he had seen her in his nightmares, a bloody, battered corpse, but as he had often seen her during the happy, carefree days of their love, her long, shining, blue-black hair swirling around her, her gold flecked eyes alive with laughter, her dainty little hands, the perfect oval of her face.

She gave him a dazzling smile.

"Welcome, my beloved. Long have I called for you, from this land out of time and space, but you were too ill, to obsessed with grief and guilt to hear me. Now you are healed. Now you love again and can let me go. Now you have found your peace and I can fully embrace the peace and the light that are my rightful legacy. Think of me, speak of me with Nerissa, for she will understand, but mourn for me no more, my beloved and remember, loved ones can leave you, but Love is everlasting."

Beatriz grazed Hunter's cheek with a feather-light touch and smiled her radiant smile again.

The light grew and grew until it became almost painful and Hunter woke, a patch of sunshine bathing his face.

He felt strangely rested, as if he had slept soundly all night long and was finally at peace.

Beatriz's smile was still with him, now an inner source of strength, and not, anymore, of sorrow.

Now he could admit it to himself - somehow, he did not know exactly when, he had fallen in love with Nerissa.

Whether he was ready to tell her, though, was an entirely different question.

Absentmindedly, Hunter let Bulwick shave him, dress him and fuss around him with unusual forbearance. The valet reminded him that, later in the afternoon, he was due for a fitting at Meyer's, his marriage being only a week hence, and, when Hunter nodded instead of grumbling and groaning, Bulwick looked at him with unfeigned surprise.

"Are you well, my lord?" he dared to ask.

Hunter looked at him with an abstract look.

"What? Yes, I am well, what is the matter with you? Stop pestering me and go ask the groom to saddle Nuage."

Relieved because his master was back to his normal, no-nonsense self, Bulwick bowed and scurried away.

Hunter could not wait to see Nerissa.

As soon as he reached Lord Chester's town house, he threw Nuage's reins to the footman who had opened the door and, without waiting to be announced, he almost ran to the library, which he knew, by now, to be Nerissa's favourite room.

The footman, a family man with a son only a few years younger than Hunter, already married and a father himself, shook his head knowingly.

"In earnest, are you?" he thought. "Good for you, our little mistress is deserving of a loving husband."

The library door was half open - Hunter peered inside and saw Nerissa sitting in front of an escritoire, her back to him, engrossed in some task he could not precisely see. Drawing, probably, he thought. The curtains were drawn back, the window open, and the room was full of light and air. He slipped cautiously through the door and crept inside, partly to surprise her, partly because he was very curious to see what she was drawing. He had his suspicions, but very much wished Nerissa to confide in him.

Stopping, he looked at Nerissa, at her long, elegant neck revealed by her upswept hair, at her creamy skin set off by her turquoise gown, at the graceful curve of her shoulders. An almost irresistible urge came upon him, to sweep her up into his arms, and kiss her breathless.

He tiptoed nearer, looked over her shoulder and was almost driven to distraction by the sight of her swelling bosom, lightly veiled by a gauze fichu.

He closed his eyes for an instant and looked again.

Nerissa was drawing a plan, and impressions of the result, for a large, magnificent formal garden, seen from different perspective angles. There were thickets and fountains, a little ornamental lake, a Greek temple on a hillock, a walled garden with wrought iron seats, where one could sit and breathe in the heady aromas of precious herbs. There were statues and urns full of flowers and winding paths flanked by herbaceous borders. There was a slender stone bridge over a brook, and a lily pond, there were deciduous and evergreen trees.

The different kinds of shrubs, trees, herbs and flowers were drawn in exquisite detail on several sheets of paper, surrounded by meticulous notes about species and varieties, the architectural elements were classically elegant, the plan as a whole was a masterpiece of balance and harmony.

Hunter could clearly perceive, just looking at it, that a stroll in that garden would be an exciting adventure, a discovery, a pleasure for the eyes and for the spirit. It was not merely craftsmanship, not even good craftsmanship - it was so far beyond that as to be art at its most complex.

The front view, including the house façade, was strangely familiar, and Hunter suddenly realised that it represented Meltonbrook Chase.

'Why,' he thought, *'the little minx!'* and was strangely moved because, it seemed, Nerissa already thought of that place as their home, hers to make into a place of harmony and beauty.

Finally understanding the scope of Nerissa's talent and the true nature of her dream, he could not stifle a gasp.

Nerissa became suddenly aware of his presence and turned, looking at him with wide, fearful eyes. A soft cry of distress escaped from her lips, while she tried to hide her drawings by turning them over.

Hunter smiled at her. "Why do you try to hide your remarkable work, Nerissa? You should be proud of it. I swear, I never saw anything so utterly fascinating. Will you explain the details to me? I must confess I do not know a thing about garden design."

Nerissa could not believe what she had just heard. He was not angry! He thought her work was remarkable! He really liked it! Her relief was so intense as to bring her near to tears.

"You do not think badly of me, then? You are not displeased?"

Hunter laughed aloud and kissed her breathless, as he had wanted to do for some time now.

Still holding her tight, he told her tenderly: "My dear, silly, wonderful Nerissa, how could I think badly of you? Besides, did you not know that Her Majesty Queen Caroline, King George II's consort, planned Hyde Park and had the Serpentine built? If a royal lady could be a garden designer, why not the wife of a simple Duke?"

"I was so afraid..." whispered Nerissa "It is such an unladylike pursuit... You know, when I was still in the schoolroom, I used to eavesdrop on my brother, Kevin's geometry lessons... I even..." she giggled, "I even... mmmh... borrowed his books, his compass and his set squares. He was very happy that he couldn't find them, for he hated geometry... This was the passion, the dream I hinted at, to you..."

"My naughty brat! Just like Kevin, anyway… I'd bet he knew perfectly well who the mysterious thief was! You must never be afraid of me, Nerissa."

Hunter went on, suddenly serious.

"This is really important for you, is it not? Well, I want you to implement your plans for Meltonbrook Chase…Yes, I recognised it, you little vixen! And, moreover, I want you to redo all of the gardens of all our estates. You have been the rage of this Season, your gardens will be the rage of the next many years, I am sure of it."

Nerissa disentangled herself from Hunter's embrace, looked at him with a Mona Lisa smile and curtsied. "Thank you, your Grace. It is a gift without price, that which you grant to me."

Hunter smiled and kissed her hands.

"I love you, Nerissa. I am the greatest fool not to have told you earlier, but somehow I did not feel I deserved you. I love you because you are what you are. I love you because you are clever, I love you because you are brave, and I love you because I know I can speak to you of anything at all and that you will understand me. I love you because you do not prattle, and because you are a talented artist, and not a boring milk and water miss, with an empty head and a vacuous smile. I could almost thank that blackguard Featherstone, whose hateful behaviour delivered you into my hands. Can I hope that one day you will love me in return?"

Nerissa stared at Hunter a moment, then suddenly flung herself at him, throwing her arms around his neck, crying and laughing at the same time.

"I love you, you thick headed clod! I have had a tendre for you since I was ten years old! I have loved you even more since my first sight of you when you came back from France and Spain. I have looked at you being pawed by half the marriageable young ladies of the *ton* and...and..."

Nerissa got no further with the sentence, as Hunter, more happy than he could have believed possible, pulled her to him, held her tight and kissed her, until they were both dizzy with the intensity of it.

Epilogue

"There, my lord…" beamed Bulwich, giving the final touches to Hunter's wedding attire.

The young Duke looked impressive in his finely tailored black superfine coat, black breeches, white silk stockings and silver brocade waistcoat. A snowy cravat, which Bulwich had insisted tying in the Ballroom style, completed his dress. "Quite delicious, my lord, I do assure you, and very becoming. The best style for a white neck cloth…"

"Do what you like, Bulwich," Hunter had answered in a tired voice. "You'll do it anyway, even if I protest!"

His friends, who were present at the dressing ceremony, had laughed immoderately.

Lord Geoffrey Clarence, who was to be Hunter's best man, gave him an ostentatious obeisance, bowing deeply and flourishing his hat.

"All hail to you, my lord Duke. I salute you! May you live happily leg-shackled for ever and ever."

"You may joke as much as you want, you wretch," grumbled Hunter. "The parson's mousetrap is waiting for all of you. The difference is that I'm marrying the fairest of them all…"

"Oh, well," quipped Lord Pendholm, "How does that saying go? All cats are grey at night… I would happily settle for a sweet natured little thing with a fat dowry… if I can find one…I am not considered a prime catch on the Marriage Mart…too many skeletons in my family's closets…"

The Hounds exchanged knowing glances. A degree of bitterness was hidden behind Charlton's jocular attitude. His departed elder brother, the former Viscount Pendholm, had been something of an unsavoury character and very unpleasant *on-dits* circulated about him.

Raphael Morton, the only Hound without a title, raised a cup of champagne and cheered. "To married bliss, dear friends! May we all find our soul mate and live happily ever after."

"Now that is a worthy and noble sentiment. Trust our plebeian friend to utter it. Long live the productive class and down with us debauched aristocrats!" guffawed Lord Barton Seddon.

"You are speaking treason, sir," laughed Hunter. "You spent too many years with them murdering Froggies, as my batman would say… Their revolutionary attitude appears to have brushed off on you."

A knock on the door interrupted the friendly banter.

"The carriage is ready, my lord." said the footman.

"Let's to church, gentlemen," said Hunter. "When we talk again, I will be a staid married man. Fancy that!"

The wedding gown had been delivered the previous evening and, on the wedding day, Madame Beaumarais herself had come to attend to the preparations. The canny Frenchwoman wanted to make sure that Lady Chester's questionable taste would not mar the wedding gown's perfection with some gaudy frill.

Pure white, which had recently come into fashion for brides, was not Nerissa's colour, but then it was not compulsory either. Thus, the couturière had been able to match the wedding gown with Nerissa's colouring and the result was spectacular. The gown was made of shimmering golden satin, the bodice delicately trimmed with green-gold lace. From the shoulders, a long train hung, in alternating matte and shiny green-gold and golden stripes. A gold filigree tiara with inset emeralds, matching earrings, green-gold elbow length gloves and green-gold satin slippers completed the ensemble.

When she saw her mistress dressed in all her finery, Lizzie, Nerissa's lady's maid, whispered in awe - "How lovely you look, my lady! You look like Springtime herself. You will outshine the sun itself today!"

"Yes, you do look wonderful, little sister. And here is your bouquet," said Kevin, presenting a square box to Nerissa. She opened it to discover a most exquisite posy of yellow roses and maidenhair fern, tied with green and golden ribbons. Nerissa gasped with pleasure and surprise.

"Thank you, my brother." She smiled mischievously. "I could throw it to you..." Kevin blanched.

"God forefend!" he exclaimed. "Father is waiting for you in the hall. May I have the honour of escorting thee thither, my lady sister?"

St. George's in Hanover Square, with its handsome neoclassical façade, was the church the *ton* bridal couples usually chose. The interior, lighted only through the beautiful stained glass windows, was dim after the bright sunlight outside.

Even if the marriage breakfast was going to be a grand affair, only the relatives and close friends of the couple attended the ceremony. Flanked by his best man, Lord Geoffrey Clarence, Hunter waited for his bride to walk down the aisle, accompanied by the solemn and joyous notes of the Trumpet Flourish by Henry Purcell. When Nerissa passed through the portal into the church, a gasp of awe escaped from everyone's lips - it was as if a sweet radiance had filled the interior, so astoundingly beautiful was the bride.

When finally Nerissa was near her groom, Lord Chester handed his daughter to Hunter and smiled. During the last few weeks, Hunter and the older gentleman had had long conversations, thanks to which Lord Chester's attitude had undergone a deep change. Talking with him, Hunter had finally understood how his war experiences could be turned into advantageous assets in managing his own land.

His flair for organisation, his attention to detail and his knack for problem solving were the stuff of which a good landowner could be made. Consequently, Lord Chester had modified the marriage agreements, granting Nerissa a much larger dowry than Hunter had ever expected.

"After all," Lord Chester had said, "you are my nearest neighbour and our lands adjoin. It goes to my advantage to have them well cared for. See my Nerissa's dowry as an investment of mine, will you? Besides, you are my best friend's boy and I have a duty towards you, have I not?"

"Dearly beloved…" the parson began and proceeded to go through the beautiful marriage service.

They exchanged their vows and, when Hunter put the wedding ring on Nerissa's finger and pronounced the age old marriage formula: *"With this ring I thee wed, with my body I thee worship, and with all my worldly goods I thee endow. In the name of the Father, and of the Son, and of the Holy Ghost. Amen."* Nerissa smiled with such shining joy that Hunter had to restrain himself from causing a scandal and kissing her there and then, without waiting for the parson's permission.

Then the recessional march began, the stirring "Rondeau" by Jean-Joseph Mouret, and the newlyweds walked down the aisle, followed by their family and friends.

Outside, Nerissa threw her bouquet and a bewildered Viscount Pendholm caught it. "Serves you right!" exclaimed Hunter, punching him on the shoulder.

A merry band, led by Kevin, was waiting for them and pelted them with a shower of rose petals and jasmine flowers.

The open carriage which would convey them back to Lord Chester's townhouse was bedecked with flowers – it would seem that their mothers' enthusiasm for excessive decoration was everywhere.

The wedding breakfast was a merry affair, with laughter, toasts and delicious food. Alyse was sitting near Lord Tillingford and, with her vivacious prattle, succeeded in making him smile and engage in light banter.

Maria, for the first time in her life, was not the fairest of them all, but was happy to leave that accolade to her sister on her wedding day. Even if she was seated near her husband, the slightly portly Lord Edmund Wollstonefort, Earl of Granville, she often stole glances at Charles, who was sitting on her left. She was finding his conversation surprisingly interesting. Today Hunter's younger brother, Viscount Wareham, looked particularly handsome, and was clearly fascinated by Nerissa's beautiful sibling, and rather puzzled that her husband appeared to pay her so little attention.

Charles and Hunter's long brother-to-brother conversations had resulted in an agreement that, for the time being, Charles would stay at Meltonbrook Chase and help Hunter to gain a better grasp of his duties as a landowner, and of the scope of his estates.

"I have too much to learn," Hunter had told Charles, "and I'd rather learn from you, than from some stiff necked steward or from some smarmy hireling." Charles had laughed. "Beware, my lord Duke! I am a very hard taskmaster!"

Sybilla was sitting near Lord Seddon, quite captured by his tales about the horses he had taken care of during the war. He talked about the exploits, the intelligence, the courage of the noble animals, showing a deep understanding and sensitivity. Sybilla, who was a very good, if somewhat reckless, horsewoman, felt an affinity with him and wondered whether, at some point in the future, they could ride together.

Perhaps here was a man who might not expect her to ride like those useless young women she so often saw riding in Hyde Park.

After the wedding breakfast, the guests gathered in the ballroom, where an orchestra was waiting for them. A lively afternoon followed, with much dancing and laughter.

The newlyweds were so patently happy together, so enthralled with each other, that nobody could doubt that they had married for love. For once, the gossips were silent. The fearsome Lady Stanmore was heard conceding that they looked very good together and ascribing to herself the merit of having brought their secret engagement into the open.

"It is the nineteenth century, after all, my dear," she told Lady Loynton. "Why should two youngsters not marry, if they are suitable and if they love each other? The age of purely arranged marriages ended a long time ago…"

The afternoon turned into evening and the guests took their leave. Soon, Nerissa went upstairs and her maid helped her to peel of her sumptuous wedding dress, to don a rather daring diaphanous nightgown, and to unbraid and brush her hair.

In his dressing room, Hunter was also undergoing preparations, assisted by Bulwich.

Once ready, he knocked the door and Nerissa opened it. The room was dimly lit by the dying embers and Nerissa's face shone like the new moon, surrounded by the golden halo of her hair. Hunter buried his hands in the silky stuff and kissed her. His hands slid down over her shoulders to the thin fabric, through which he could feel her smooth, firm flesh, free at last from stays and bulky gowns.

Daringly, Nerissa undid the belt of his silk banyan and gasped, discovering that he was not wearing a nightgown.

"Fie, sir!" she complained, laughing. "Are you not ashamed?"

"Come here, wife," growled Hunter, also laughing at the expression on her face. "You've teased me long enough!"

Willingly, she came into his arms, and they kissed, again and again, their hands exploring, their bodies entwined, as the garments they had been wearing slid to the floor in a discarded heap.

(You'll find a taste of book 2, "Intriguing the Viscount" just after the 'About the Author' section in this book!)

Arietta Richmond
Regency Historical Romance

About the Author

Arietta Richmond has been a compulsive reader and writer all her life. Whilst her reading has covered an enormous range of topics, history has always fascinated her, and historical novels been amongst her favourite reading.

She has written a wide range of work, from business articles and other non-fiction works (published under a pen name) but fiction has always been a major part of her life. Now, her Regency Historical Romance books are finally being released. The Derbyshire Set is comprised of 10 shorter novels (6 released so far). The 'His Majesty's Hounds' series is comprised of 10 novels, with the fifth having just been released.

She also has a standalone longer novel shortly to be released, and two other series of novels in development.

She lives in Australia, and when not reading or writing, likes to travel, and to see in person the places where history happened.

Be the first to know about it when Arietta's next book is released!

Sign up to Arietta's newsletter at

http://www.ariettarichmond.com

When you do, you will receive a free copy of the <u>subscriber exclusive</u> novella **'A Gift of Love',** a prequel to the Derbyshire Set series, which ends on the day that 'The Earl's Unexpected Bride' begins

This story is not for sale anywhere – it is absolutely exclusive to newsletter subscribers!

Here is your preview of the next book in the 'His Majesty's Hounds' series by Arietta Richmond

His Majesty's Hounds – Book 2

Sweet and Clean Regency Romance

Intriguing the Viscount

Arietta Richmond

Chapter 1

London lay under a deep cover of snow, but everyone seemed to share a feeling of carefree happiness. This was the first Christmas after the end of the long Napoleonic Wars. Waterloo, the mother of all battles, had ended with a resounding victory and, after many years spent fighting, the surviving soldiers had returned to their homes. For most, there was much to celebrate this Christmas, and choirs could sing "Glory to God in the highest, and on earth peace, good will toward men!" giving full value to the truth of the joyous words. But for some, that joy was tempered by other concerns…

Offering his arm to his mother, Lady Pendholm, Lord Charlton Edgeworth, Viscount Pendholm, entered Lord Baildon's townhouse. A footman hurried to relieve them of their outer garments.

They joined the receiving line, and soon they were announced, and went on to join the crush in the ballroom.

Their appearance was followed by a sudden hush, after which conversations resumed, with a slight edge to them. Nobody knew a lot about the new Lord Pendholm, who had only recently returned from the wars on the Continent, to resume his life, and to succeed his brother, the former Viscount Pendholm, who had died in a rather scandalous way, a few months previously.

It was common knowledge, among the *ton*, that the deceased Lord Pendholm had been something of an unsavoury character. His prowess as a gambler was legendary and it was whispered that he had not restricted himself to respectable gentlemen's clubs like White's or Watier's, but had also attended disreputable gaming hells, associating with shady personages, usurers, swindlers, crooks and all manner of riff raff.

Another, darker rumour circulated among the gentlemen: that the late Lord Pendholm had had a nasty penchant for violence against women. All of the demi-monde had suddenly ostracised him, after he had viciously beaten a famed *soi-disant* French courtesan, and Mrs Tennant, a notorious Abbess, had banned him from her house of pleasure. All these juicy tit-bits were whispered behind fans and in dark corners, while Charlton and his mother circulated amongst the guests.

Lady Pendholm was in her early fifties and still a beautiful woman. She was silver haired and slender and her son knew well that, under an air of refined gentility, she hid the resilience of a steel blade, the same quality that flashed in her greenish brown eyes when she perceived how they were being oh-not-so-very-subtly snubbed by the *ton*.

She lightly squeezed Charlton's arm, a silent warning not to react. Lord Pendholm looked around, to see if any of his friends were there, but he knew that was a forlorn hope.

Lord Hunter Barrington, Duke of Melton, was spending Christmas with his family at Meltonbrook Chase and would arrive later, at the beginning of the Season; Mr Raphael Morton, as a wealthy Cit, was not normally invited to the *ton*'s entertainments, despite the very real fact that he could buy off many an aristocrat, with change to spare; Lord Geoffrey Clarence was undoubtedly suffering under the grinding heel of his brother, Lord Alfred Clarence, Marquess Woodford, who was rather forcefully focussed on educating poor Geoff in his responsibilities as his heir; Lord Barton Seddon and Lord Gerald Otford, Baron Tillingford were off somewhere together, probably buying horses to improve Gerry's stock at his new estates.

Charlton sighed. The unlikely group known as His Majesty's Hounds had formed during the war, as a very select unit, a closely knit association of men of different, and priceless, talents. Their friendship had been forged on the anvil of many harrowing experiences and was invaluable for all of them. It was second nature for each of them to look for the other Hounds when in any difficult situations, or when faced with potential conflict. And this, his first public appearance at a social function since his return, was making Charlton feel on edge, his perceptions keenly alert, all of his fighting instincts to the fore.

He smiled bleakly. This first skirmish, though important, was not decisive by any means.

He had many battles ahead to fight and win, if he wanted his family to regain the social standing they'd once had and which his brother's behaviour had called into question.

And win he would, Charlton vowed: Harriet, his baby sister, a lively, spirited, pretty young thing, would not be looked at askance. He was an honourable man, from an honourable line: he would not allow one rotten apple to ruin it for them all.

Something caught Charlton's attention, pulling him out of his thoughts, and into the moment. Maybe because he was thinking about war, it seemed significant - it was a man, somewhat older than Charlton, a slim, elegant figure, clad entirely in black, with a ruby signet ring on his finger and a sharp, aquiline profile.

It was the ring that created the association in Charlton's mind. It was the same ring, or a very similar one, as he had once seen on the hand of a man who had been pointed out to him as a French agent. Was it really him? And, if so, whatever was he doing in London, attending a Christmas ball?

As he considered the puzzle of the mysterious guest, the crowd parted, revealing a young lady standing beside an older one and looking around with a half excited, half scared expression. A simile flashed through Charlton's mind - the shell opens to reveal the pearl.

He paused, looking at her, and the crowd vanished, the noise quieted, time itself stopped. She was petite, but lushly curved, with a heart shaped face, a small pointed chin, a pert upturned nose and a wide brow with perfect, dark, wing shaped eyebrows.

Her skin was as translucent as mother of pearl, her eyes reminded him of the colour of the gentian violets he had once seen on the Swiss Alps, before the war. She was tastefully dressed in a jonquil satin gown, trimmed with white lace, elbow length white gloves and dainty white kid slippers.

A bony lady in Pomona green elbowed him as she moved through the crush, and brought him out of his reverie. After a perfunctory "Your pardon, my Lady", and without losing track of the unknown enchantress, Charlton looked for his mother, in the hope that she might know her, and therefore be able to introduce him.

Lady Pendholm was talking with her long-time friend Sir Arthur Bowscale, a distinguished gentleman in his sixties, who owned a ramshackle mansion near Pendholm Hall, their country seat, and who, thanks to his acquaintance with a number of influential peers, had been able to smooth over most the unpleasantness and the scandal following Michael's murder.

Lady Pendholm looked at her son and was surprised to see the normally calm and steady young man fidgeting.

"Did you want to speak with me, my son?" she asked graciously, her expression curious.

"Yes, Mother, if you please. Would you be as kind as to tell me whether you happen to know that young lady over there, the one dressed in jonquil satin?"

Lady Pendholm peered through her quizzing glass.

"The one near the portly lady in slate grey?"

"Yes Mother, that one. Do you know her?"

"Hmmm, no, I do not think so. I have never seen her before, which is strange. I thought I knew almost everybody. The *ton*, after all, is the most parochial group I know. My curiosity is piqued. Come, my son, let us look for our hostess and ask her."

Lady Catharine Baildon, a vivacious and slightly garrulous sixtyish woman, was chatting with Lady Magda Wilmson, and telling her, in painstaking detail, all about her younger nephew's exploits and vagaries.

"My dearest Sylvia!" she gushed. "How nice to see you again, after your terrible ordeal… and here is Lord Pendholm… What a handsome gentleman you have become, my dear Charlie! Excuse me if I seem overfamiliar, but I saw you in your swaddling clothes and you will allow an old woman her vagaries… So, you are back from the wars, at long last, and high time it was for that beastly Frenchman to be bundled up and sent halfway to nowhere to live or to die as he pleases… We must find a nice girl for you straight away, my lord, you need to settle down and have a few children of your own… Will it not be a treat, my dear Sylvia, to hold a baby again, all warm and cuddly? I dote on my Eddie's brood… five of them, up to now, and I could swear dear Dorothy - you know, Eddie's wife – is breeding again…" Half amused and half vexed, Lady Pendholm succeeded at last in stemming her friend's seemingly unstoppable flow of words.

"Will you indulge my curiosity, my dear Catharine? You know that I have been out of society for more than eighteen months now, in our time of mourning - you must bring me up to date. Nobody is as knowledgeable as you are about what is going on with the *ton*. For instance, who are those two ladies over there? I cannot seem to remember them."

Lady Baildon, who was very short-sighted but too vain to use a quizzing glass, squinted. "The young one in jonquil satin is Lady Odette Marmont, and the older one in slate grey is her aunt, Lady Farnsworth. Poor Odette has no mother to look after her - orphaned, you know – and Lady Farnsworth - her mother's sister, you know – is chaperoning her. Almost on the shelf, she is. Already twenty-two and not even betrothed. Very shy little mousy thing, not spirited at all. Would you like me to introduce you?"

Lady Pendholm smiled. One could always count on Catharine for a bit of harmless meddling.

"If you would be so kind, I would be delighted, I'm sure."

With the majesty of a frigate under full sail, Lady Baildon ploughed through the crowd, with Charlton and his mother in tow, and reached Lady Farnsworth and Lady Odette.

Seeing their hostess approaching them, Odette opened her eyes wide and seemed on the point of bolting, but Lady Farnsworth put a restraining hand on her elbow and hissed "Are you set on disgracing me, you wretched girl? Behave yourself! You are not a cowering, mistreated scullery maid, you are a Lady and like a Lady will you comport yourself. Now, stop fidgeting, stand straight and try to be gracious."

"Good evening, Lady Farnsworth, how are you? I would like to introduce you to a very dear friend of mine, Lady Sylvia Edgeworth, Viscountess Pendholm. And this is her son, Charlton Edgeworth, Viscount Pendholm. You might have heard that his elder brother, the former Lord Pendholm, died of late. They are just out of mourning and re-acquainting themselves with society life."

Lady Farnsworth smiled. She was a formidable looking woman, with a white streak in her dark hair, piercing grey eyes, a strong chin and an imposing Roman nose.

"My dear Lady Pendholm, how do you do? I do feel for you, my dear husband died not long ago and, between war and mourning, we have not been attending society for a long time. Lord Pendholm, I am honoured to meet you. I'm told you are a war hero and that all of us should be grateful to you for having rid us of the Scourge of Europe. May I introduce you to my dear niece, Lady Odette Marmont? She is the daughter of my dear departed sister. She is here with her father, the Comte de Vierzon. French aristocracy suffered many indignities at the hands of the Corsican parvenu and rejoice with us at his defeat."

Odette looked at Charlton and, caught by his gaze, had to restrain herself from staring.

He was a very handsome gentleman, with his wavy locks the colour of a ripe chestnut, rich with golden highlights, and his rich, warm chocolate eyes, where golden motes danced, but what Odette perceived was a compelling quality about him, a feeling of energy held on a tight leash, a strong magnetism emanating from the core of his being. He was the most intensely alive person that Odette had ever encountered.

While Odette and Charlton looked at each other, their wits askew, the three older ladies were engaged in a lively chat.

"Do you see the black clad gentleman over there, the one talking with Lord Stanmore? He is Odette's father, the Comte de Vierzon."

Charlton snapped out of his besotted trance and looked at Odette's father. It was with deep disquiet that he recognised the gentleman he had previously noted. A French agent? An enemy spy? Or simply a French aristocrat, reinstated to his rightful standing by Napoleon's defeat?

'It is not my issue to worry about anymore,' he thought. *'Now I have other fish to fry'.* Yet the sense of disquiet remained, even as he found his gaze drawn, irresistibly it seemed, back to the remarkable blue violet of Lady Odette's eyes.

Get

"Intriguing the Viscount"

as soon as it's released – go to

http://www.ariettarichmond.com

and make sure that you are signed up for news and release notices !

Books in the 'His Majesty's Hounds' Series

Redeeming the Marquess (coming soon)

Healing Lord Barton (coming soon)

Winning the Merchant Earl (coming soon)

Loving the Bitter Baron (coming soon)

Rescuing the Countess (coming soon)

Attracting the Spymaster (coming soon)

Books in 'The Derbyshire Set'

Available at all good book stores and for ebook readers too!

Coming Soon!

Other Books from Dreamstone Publishing

Dreamstone publishes books in a wide variety of categories – here are some of our other bestselling books:-

We have books in many categories, ranging from Erotica and Romance to Kids Books, Books on Writing, Business Books, Photography, Cook Books, Diaries, Coloring books and much more. New books are released each month.

Be the first to know when our next books are coming out

Be first to get all the news – sign up for our newsletter at

http://www.dreamstonepublishing.com

www.ingramcontent.com/pod-product-compliance
Lightning Source LLC
Chambersburg PA
CBHW060804210726
48292CB00013B/1755